WHITE DEATH

By Ted Bell

Fiction
WARRIORS
PHANTOM
WARLORD
TSAR
SPY
PIRATE
ASSASSIN
HAWKE

Coming Soon in Hardcover
PATRIOT

Novellas
WHAT COMES AROUND
CRASH DIVE
WHITE DEATH

Children's Books
THE TIME PIRATE
NICK OF TIME

WHITE DEATH

An Alex Hawke Novella

TED BELL

WITNESS
IMPULSE
An Imprint of HarperCollinsPublishers

Excerpt from *Patriot* copyright © 2015 by Theodore A. Bell.

EPub Edition JULY 2015 ISBN: 9780062283221

Print Edition ISBN: 9780062415431

10 9 8 7 6

CHAPTER ONE

The Swiss Alps

It is often said that our greatest strength is also our greatest weakness. Lieutenant Christian Hartz, Tenth Mountain Division, Swiss Army, was about to learn firsthand the terrible truth of that dusty old bit of wisdom. The lesson would be taught to this young fellow by a mountain. Der Nadel, an infamous Swiss Alp, was known to climbers around the world by its nickname, "White Death." And for very good reason.

Christian toe-pointed the spiked crampons strapped to his boots into the vertical wall of sheer ice. He was able to kick the steel spikes at the toes of his boots a good two inches in. His lower body secure, he then secured his upper torso, swinging his ice ax into the wall above his head, and then a second ax to lock him in. Firmly wed to the mountain, he leaned back and looked straight up.

The towering vertical slab of ice and rock soared high into the clouds above him, finally disappearing into swirling grey mists that haunted the peak almost daily. He started moving again.

At this point, the summit of the mountain was 15,330 feet

above his head. Roughly three miles straight up. The summit of Der Nadel was at 25,430 feet above sea level. It was called "The Needle" because of the thin, twisted spire that scratched the sky at the summit. Attempting to scale that spire had killed more climbers than any other mountain in Switzerland.

So far, the lieutenant's moves had not been technically difficult. Still, the climbing was causing him continuous insecurity due to the *foehnsturms* swirling about him as he went higher. A *foehn* is a downslope wind that occurs in the lee, or downwind, side of a high mountain range, like the moist winds off the Mediterranean Sea that sweep up over the Alps.

Recent weather from the north had brought winds of eighty-plus miles per hour, subzero temperatures, ice, and the relentless blinding snow. Still, Hartz had made good progress.

The wide ledge on which he now stood, very secure for the moment, was known as "Das Boot." The mammoth rock formation looked as if some giant battleship's entire bow section had suddenly blasted through the rock and now protruded from the mountain at ten thousand feet. A good place for tea. The lieutenant fired up his little stove and melted some snow in his pot. Earl Grey had never tasted so good.

The good-looking soldier had been sent up the hill to find, and bring safely down, a lone climber, a young Italian woman who'd spent the night on a fingernail of rock, suffering in the ninety-plus-mile-per-hour winds and ice. For a long time, this climber had been the focus of the ranger station's high-powered optics.

When dawn broke she was gone. She'd either fallen,

pitched forward into a hidden crevasse, or descended safely to a spot now hidden from sight. Lieutenant Hartz's job was to find out which one was true and bring her down. Due to weather, the chances that she was still alive and fighting for her survival were slim. But there was a chance.

Christian reached up, stretching his body to the limit so his fingers could feel along the smooth face. He was looking for the next place where he could sink a pick or a cam so he could haul himself up the next pitch. He felt strong, but he'd been climbing since first light and it had been painfully slow going, mostly due to the increasing winds and dropping temperatures as he gained altitude.

Five long hours later, his lats, biceps, and triceps were screaming in unison, and he hadn't even reached the hard part yet. But he knew it was coming. The hard part was next. The hard part was the north face of Der Nadel, otherwise known as the "Murder Wall."

The infamous vertical face had long been called that, and for good reason. It was the last big hurdle one had to overcome before attacking the imposing summit. Of all those who'd risked their lives to conquer this final ascent, many had served, but few had been chosen.

Lieutenant Hartz, now just twenty-seven years old, had been acclaimed the highest-ranking alpinist in his entire army division. He was proud of that. When he'd told his mum about it, she'd cried. He was number one out of some ten thousand Swiss soldiers, all of whom, like him, had been born on skis with axes in their hands—highly skilled young men, fiercely determined, in peak condition for physical and mental strength, extreme high-altitude climbing, and, most important of all, supreme confidence. That was your ticket up the hill.

His timing couldn't have been worse. One of the most violent storms to rip through the canton in nearly a decade had arrived as if on cue. And he was on a time crunch. The lost climber's rescue clock had started ticking long before the first swing of his ice ax at dawn to begin his ascent.

The woman could no longer be seen. She'd been on a narrow ledge, high on the Murder Wall. She was now out of sight and out of communication range. Aerial searches by helicopters had not been successful, and the weather had finally grounded them. The young woman's last transmission had indicated she'd been gravely injured but was determined to survive. "I'll hold on," she had promised, "but please come soon!"

Christian's division commander had espoused a theory that the woman might well have found one of the old wooden escape doors built into the side of the mountain. Behind these doors were safety tunnels bored into the mountain over the centuries. The problem was that there were countless numbers of these doors up there, invisible flyspecks spread across the massive north face.

Classic needle in a haystack, Christian thought. His *divisionnaire,* Baron Wolfgang von Stuka, known behind his back as "Wolfie," had summoned Christian to his office just after midnight, given him the brief, and said, "Lieutenant, please get your ass up there, *and find that young woman!*"

And here he was.

Darkness was closing in. It was now past five o'clock on that brutally cold grey afternoon in December. Lieutenant Hartz, trying to reach the same narrow ledge where the climber had last been seen, was struggling a bit. He was currently in the midst of an upward traverse across the lower sections of that sheer wall so smooth that it appeared almost polished. This part, the hard part, was challenging to the world's very best climbers. And he was only best in his Swiss Army division.

"Imagine climbing a couple of miles up a slightly cracked mirror looking for invisible cracks," was how his Tenth Mountain Division instructors had explained it to the new cadets. That message had sunk in with many of them, but many had not listened. Tales of the Tenth Division versus the Murder Wall were legend. The number of cadets who'd died up there was a closely guarded secret.

One that no one wanted to know.

Chapter Two

In the 1930s, sporting climbers from all over the world began flocking to Switzerland as word of the impossible face spread. They came in droves, determined to conquer the needle-like summit. Topping out at 25,430 feet, Der Nadel ranked with Everest and K2 as one of the deadliest mountains in the world. In a storm like this, it was *the* deadliest. Since the first climbers had attempted to conquer the north face in 1933, over seventy-five men had died up there. Countless had been severely injured. And almost everyone lucky enough to survive had never gone anywhere near Der Nadel again.

By the time Lieutenant Hartz had climbed one thousand feet, insecurity had given way to the first hints of panic.

Hartz paused to hammer in another titanium tube into the coat of ice. He missed the target and his hammer careened off the rock. He felt himself starting to shake. The hardened steel trap that was the young soldier's mind was beginning to crack under the strain. Cracks just wide enough to admit slivers of fear.

Determined to fulfill his mission, Hartz kept climbing,

his fingers searching for purchase as new layers of thin ice coating made it ever more difficult. He swung his ice ax again and again, looking for another pick. His normally icy nerves continued to unravel with each swing of the ax.

He realized he was now sweating profusely despite the subzero temperatures at that altitude, something he'd never done before. His bowels were dangerously close to the boiling point. He knew why. It was because he was now passing by certain early but prominent landmarks of Der Nadel. Crumbling outcroppings, ragged formations, rotten ice, all had given him nightmares as a young boy thumbing through his alpine picture books, dreaming of climbing and the Swiss Army.

Crabbing gingerly across the broad slab of ice, he found that the wall steepened, the snow cover thinned, and his ice ax ricocheted off solid rock a few inches beneath the crust. With the advent of rotten ice at the higher elevations, Christian now felt a nauseous anxiety that shook him to the core.

He felt the only thing preventing him cartwheeling off into space was a pair of two thin titanium bolts sunk half an inch into rotten ice. Ice that looked like the inside of his freezer when it badly needed defrosting. Then came the first truly stupid mistake of the day.

Lieutenant Hartz looked down.

He saw the ground spinning more than nine thousand feet below. And suddenly felt woozy, even dizzy, as if he was about to faint. He wrestled mightily for control of his once stalwart mind and took a dozen deep breaths before he could resume climbing. Normally, his steely confidence made short work of encroaching panic, crowding it out. It had been his greatest strength. Now he wondered if it would soon become his downfall.

This time, to his mounting horror, everything was different.

It had taken him six tortured hours to climb a mere forty-eight hundred feet up the face. Hartz figured he had maybe three more hours of reasonable daylight to reach the roughly calculated area he'd been assigned to scout for a survivor.

The weather was deteriorating so rapidly that he was at the point where it looked as if he might soon be needing that rescue door himself.

He paused to check his altimeter, and a new kind of fear crept into his reeling mind on silent tiptoes. Based on his current rate of ascent, he knew that only two scenarios were now even possible. One, best case, he'd actually find the door, and the climber behind it would be alive. He'd take shelter inside the mountain with her for the night. Ride out the storm and get her down next morning. But it was a night that promised nothing good. It was already shaping up to be wretched from any perspective.

Foehnsturms, heavy snowfall, and high winds were increasing the chance of avalanches and thundering rock slides by a factor of ten. Worst case? He might never even reach the altitude where he might *find* that door, much less rescue anybody.

If worst did prove to be the case, it meant he'd have to stop climbing and soon. He'd need somewhere, anywhere, to spend the night; perched on some craggy overhang, some random narrow ledge where he could huddle against the rock, totally unprotected from the raging elements.

An even worse scenario? There would be no ledge at all. He would be forced to hang suspended from two anchors embedded perhaps one-quarter of an inch into crumbly rock and ice. Hanging in space and twisting in a violent, icy wind. An entire night of darkness, dangling at ten thousand feet in the middle of a Category 4 hurricane.

He shook his head and tried to clear his trembling mind.

He had little choice but to continue moving up the face. Duty dictated that decision. But the longer he climbed, and the wearier and more unsure he grew, the more he began to question the wisdom of his decision to keep on going. He was moving at a snail's pace, doing a long end run around yet another wide ledge protruding from the rock just above him.

He felt dizzy, like he might faint. He had to take a few minutes' rest before he could resume climbing. When he resumed, he tried to regain his focus by thinking of something else, anything else, as he moved upward across the face. After half an hour, he came within sight of a familiar landmark above.

His platoon called that imposing strip awning of rock "der Flughafen." In English, that meant "the airport." The departure lounge to the Eternal Kingdom. God's waiting room. If it was a joke, as some people said, he didn't get it. There was nothing remotely amusing about getting under that damn overhang before you even had a shot at climbing on top of it!

The crumbling rock wall here was coated with two inches

of ice. Thin though the layer was, it was still enough to hold his ice ax in place if he swung it slowly. He kept moving, praying for any change in his luck. He was certainly due one. And that's when he saw an old, frayed rope someone had left behind. A line that emerged intermittently from the glazing and continued upward across the face.

Some long-ago climber he'd never know had left him a lifeline.

Nearly paralyzed with fear and desperate for anything at all that might subdue his mounting panic, Christian was shamelessly, and very dangerously, grabbing at bits of old rope whenever they were visible. Any slip now would send him plummeting to the bottom of the wall, eight thousand feet of free fall with no chute and no God to save him.

He went higher, foolishly holding his breath to calm a deepening anxiety he'd never known before. Now he started thinking that his much-vaunted confidence had put him up here. And now that that same cocksure attitude that had been his lifelong cornerstone was going to send him to his death, he could almost feel his confidence seeping out through his pores.

Still, he climbed higher toward his objective, looking for each new shred of frayed rope, literally grasping at straws as he scaled the Murder Wall.

CHAPTER THREE

The whole spectrum of the face was in atrocious condition, far worse than he'd expected. It was plastered with rime and loaded with unstable snow. He was now officially shit out of luck. There was nowhere left to go now, no place to— He saw the rope dangling two feet away! He lunged for it, and that's when he made the worst mistake of his short life.

He made a single misstep in a game where that's all it took. Both of his ice axes and the spiky crampons on his boots sheared out of the rotten ice at the same moment.

Hartz found himself airborne, the wind tearing at his clothes as he hurtled downward.

They say time slows down just before you die. That you revisit all the important scenes from your life, like a movie. It's all bullshit. You fall off a mountaintop and three seconds later you're a bug on the windshield of life.

He only knew he was alive because his eyes popped open on the world. He pinched his mind to see if this could be real.

He was numbingly cold and couldn't feel his feet, but he tried moving his leg and succeeded. It was real. Slowly, painfully, he lifted his head from the powdery snow and surveyed his immediate surroundings. Ice, rock, sky. How in God's name had he gotten here? Moving his arms and legs to increase circulation, he soon discovered the reason for his miraculous salvation.

Incredibly, he'd landed on a ledge he'd not known even existed. He'd fallen at least five hundred feet when the frayed rope had parted. He could almost make out the bitter end of it twisting in the wind high above him. Had rock ice or granite been below him, he would have died instantly. Instead, his landing had been cushioned by a heavy accumulation of crushed and powdery snow. The stuff must have been falling hard while he'd been struggling up there, fearing for his future.

God had saved him after all. He lay there for a long while, thanking everybody up there and thinking of his small family. Sandra, Willy, and his dog, Ludwig, waiting for him to come home to them that night. That he would see his wife and daughter again seemed a miracle. He lay there like that for a long time, exhausted, dreaming of home, and fell asleep with a smile on his face. After a while, he woke and felt himself strong enough and reasonably clear-headed enough to climb out of the snowbank and start looking for a feasible route of descent. The weather and ice prohibited going further. He snapped on the halogen light on his helmet, miraculously still there. Slowly, he made his way lower. He'd been able to walk away from the fall with no more damage than bruises and a painful crimp in his back.

The sharp back pain actually helped him keep alert. Presently, he came to a yawning crevasse he would certainly have stumbled into had it not been for the powerful headlamp. Now, carefully retracing his steps and circumventing the crevasse, his crampons gave him good traction across the treacherous ice field. He picked his way down with his ax, seeing some of the same holds he'd used on the way up.

He had been climbing downward for about a half hour when he crested a broad slab of ice. He saw something that caused him to think he really was losing his mind. He blinked his eyes, sure he was still delusional from the panic attack and the fall. Because what he saw atop a mound of snow a few feet below his feet defied all logic.

It was a head. Not a skull but a decapitated human *head*. With a pair of horn-rimmed sunglasses buried in the snow a few feet away.

The head was perched almost playfully atop a large snowdrift. There was a thin crust of ice on the head's face. Christian knelt down on one knee and studied his find more carefully. He clawed some crusty ice away, trying to free the head from the ice beneath the jaw. But it had frozen. The dead man's head was cemented in place.

He could see it was a male; the features were still discernible. Caucasian. The nose misshapen from a fall. Dark blond hair matted with dark black blood. Not an old guy, maybe early forties. The mouth, too, was frozen, opened in a permanent rictus of scream. The teeth were all shattered or missing. The blue eyes had also locked up in the open position.

The most bizarre thing of all? There was a total absence of tracks in the snow around the head. No signs of foul play, nor any footprints anywhere near the vicinity. A freak snowfall?

Yet now there was this human head, sitting on the snow. And a pair of eyeglasses.

Impossible.

But that was exactly what he saw.

The following is the missing persons report Lieutenant Hartz filed with Swiss Army Military Police at Zurich HQ immediately upon his return from his failed rescue attempt in the southern Alps:

> Male, Caucasian, approximately forty years of age, close-cropped blond hair, light blue eyes, two-inch scar on the left cheek. Teeth broken or missing. Massive contusion inside the hairline at the right temple. Left ear missing. No further evidence or descriptions possible at this time.
>
> (Signed) Lieutenant Christian Hartz 10th Mountain Div., Swiss Army

Chapter Four

London

"God how I hate these bloody things," Chief Inspector Ambrose Congreve said. He was struggling to keep both his putter and his spindly golf umbrella under control in an unexpected blizzard. Nearly white-out conditions were not ideal for his golf score.

Lord Alexander Hawke, who much preferred the name Alex, smiled at his old golf partner and even older friend, a currently snow-coated former Scotland Yard chief inspector. "Would you mind putting, Constable? I mean, while we're still young?"

"I can't bloody see the bloody hole, can I?" Congreve shouted with a trace of frustration.

"So what? You can't get it in even when you *can* see the bloody hole. So, putt!"

It was December, a Saturday. A day on which no sane man in England would venture out onto a golf course. But Ambrose Congreve and Alex Hawke made no claims regarding their sanity. Only their passion for the grand old game of golf dictated their actions.

A coating of light snow and frost had painted the trees and the fairways a fairy-tale white. The sudden sight of nasty weather had made one of them inexplicably cheery. And the other rather not.

The two sportsmen were on the treacherous fifth green at Hawke's beloved Sunningdale Golf Club just north of London—a difficult par four, and the bane of Inspector Congreve's existence, most especially on this particularly insalubrious Saturday morning.

Congreve, who carried his weight around his circumference, was attempting to squat down and line up his putt, somewhat in the manner of Tiger Woods. The new Tiger, not the old Tiger. Suffice it to say, it was not a pretty sight.

And that sudden wind had come, howling up and down the wide fairway. And the icy particles. And the blinding snow. Hawke, who'd always nursed a secret love of foul weather, was stoic, braving the gale-force winds, standing rooted to the snowy green, his frozen putter in his hand and a smile frozen on his face. He was watching Ambrose struggle with his wild umbrella, trying to keep his footing on the treacherous ice. "Perhaps the hurricane will simply loft you and your errant brolly up and away, into the heavens, just like Mary Poppins in the Disney film of the same name," he said.

Ambrose shouted above the wind, "And hopefully I'll be dropped off somewhere near the bloody clubhouse! Hopefully in the middle of the men's grill room. There's a crackling fire blazing in the hearth right now, you know, Alex. Warmth, whisky, and not a wife in sight."

"Shut up and putt, Ambrose."

"Then get out of the way, will you, you're standing directly in my line!" Congreve cried above the wind, waving putter and umbrella around in a rage of frustration.

Hawke said, "How am I supposed to know where your line is when it's covered with snow!"

They were the only twosome either brave enough, or foolish enough, to be out on the links this frightfully wintry morning. Fiendishly icy winds and wet snow were terrorizing the few souls who'd not retreated to the grill.

Congreve's putt was well wide of the mark. It slid thirty feet past the cup, gathered speed on a sheet of black ice, narrowly missed a frozen water hazard, then trickled down into the snow-filled sand trap. He would now be hitting an eight.

"May I?" Hawke said, standing over his nearly invisible ball, which lay three. He was looking at Congreve deferentially, but with just a tinge of schadenfreude.

"Just putt."

Lord Hawke promptly sank a smashing fifteen-footer, even though he couldn't see it disappear into a slight depression that had marked the cup's location.

"Four! That's a par!" Hawke said, pumping his fist in the air as he bent down to pluck his ball from the hole.

"Par?" Ambrose snorted. "Surely you did not say the *par* word, Alex. Hardly a par, my dear boy. Bogie or double bogie at the very best."

Hawke was indignant. "Count them. Drive into the middle of the fairway, lying one. No mulligan. Two into the fairway trap. Three, chipped onto the green. Four, sank the putt. Par."

"Not four, Alex, not even close. Let me think about it. Six. Yes. Take at least a six on the card while I consider the sequence of salient events for a moment."

Hawke could hear the wheels spinning as Congreve cogitated beneath his umbrella. He could never fathom how the world-famous criminalist could work his brain so fast and deep that no other man in the country could touch him.

Whenever anyone inquired about the contents of his cranium, the man would lift his great head and say, "It's not my brain at all, it's the lower nerve center. That's the base of operations."

Whatever that meant.

"I was right," the rotund detective said. "Bogie. Take a five. Even though it was arguably a six or seven."

"I certainly will not take a five, I am not about to let you . . . hold on a tick. My mobile's humming."

"You can't take a call on the course, Alex. There's a loo up on top of that hill. Go up there before you get us thrown off this hallowed ground!" Hawke ascended the hill.

"What took you so long? I'm bloody freezing," Ambrose said when Hawke came trudging back down through knee-deep snow.

"The telephone call, you mean? Oh, Sir David calling from the office, on a secure line. You won't like it one bit."

"Try me."

"Another last-minute summons from my esteemed employer at MI6. Of course, while we're out enjoying a fine Saturday morning on the links, he's helming the great ship of state from his desk by the Thames, hell-bent on making the rest of us poor serfs feel guilty."

"I don't feel guilty in the slightest. And I would opine that the chief of British Secret Services takes great delight in toying with you, Alex. Playing you like his star fiddle."

"Not even remotely true."

"What's the old man on about this time?"

"Something about a murder in Zurich. Impacts state security, that's all. Very hush-hush about the whole affair, as befits his station. Wants us, yes, you too, to meet him for cocktails in London at his club, Boodle's, at five."

"Fine. Wonderful. Why in God's name do I have to come? He's your boss, not mine, thank heavens. I've other things to do, frankly. My wife expects me home at two to help her can peaches."

"Sad, no? Sir David said he might well be in need of that monumental brain and those legendary detective skills before whatever nasty business that awaits us is over. What it's really all about, he neglected to say—what time is it? We'd better get on the road. As you know, he abhors tardiness."

They headed for the car park and Alex's steel-grey 1957 Bentley Continental. A mammoth beast he called "the Locomotive."

"If we're late," Congreve said, "just use that lethal smile of yours to charm the birds out of his trees."

"Tried it many times. His birds have all flown the coop."

Lord Hawke had charm to spare. He stood well north of six feet. He had a full head of unruly black hair and crystalline blue eyes that some London gossip queen had once referred to in print as "pools of frozen arctic rain." People of every stripe and gender found him attractive. As was often said of him, "Men wanted to stand him a drink, while women much preferred him horizontal."

For a gentleman in his midthirties, he was in splendid shape. His nearby country estate, five miles from the Sunningdale links, was called Hawkesmoor. He had a stable of race cars, a boxing ring where he sparred, a shooting range where he shot, and a hall where he fenced. He swam six miles in open ocean whenever he got the chance and did laps in the indoor pool at home when he did not.

But it was his easygoing manner, matched with fierce determination, a keen moral sense, and courage under fire that made him the most valued and successful counterterror officer in the entire British Secret Service.

Many had, over the years, underestimated Alex Hawke, this gentleman spy, at their peril, and many had paid full measure for that mistake. He was, when all was said and done, a dashing and aristocratic English nobleman, of noble principles, who could kill you using only one of his bare hands.

CHAPTER FIVE

"Ah, there you are, Sir David!" Hawke said, feigning over-whelming joy at the sight of the man he worked for, a stern-looking gentleman in a blue worsted suit who awaited them on a curving red leather banquette. He was in his usual spot, nursing a light whisky soda in a quiet corner of the Men's Grille at the London gentlemen's club in St. James known as Boodle's.

"Oh, hullo. You look bloody awful," C said to Hawke, inspecting him up and down.

"We try."

"You should never again be seen in public wearing those tartan golfing slacks again. Tartan! Painful. It reflects badly upon me and on the entire Secret Service."

"With all due respect, I'd intended to spend the day at the golf course, not in a London gentlemen's club, sir."

Trulove waved the excuse away.

"Time is wasting," he said. "Sit down, both of you, and have a drink. You both look like you could use one. A pair of drowned rats, soaked to the skin!"

"Rats?" Congreve whispered out of the corner of his mouth, certain he'd misunderstood the word.

"What can I offer you, Inspector Congreve?" C said. "I caught you looking rather longingly at the barman over there."

"Oh. Was I really?"

"Name your poison, Chief Inspector."

"Macallan's single malt, if you have it, if not, Dewar's, please," Ambrose smiled. "It never varies, you know. Believe me, I speak from vast experience."

"And for you, Alex?"

"Rum, please. A tot of Gosling's Black Seal if you don't mind. The 151 proof."

Sir David repeated their requests to the club steward and added a glass of Margaux for himself. When the drinks were in hand, he raised his glass and said, "*Slange var*! A Gaelic toast meaning 'Get it to the hole!'"

"*Slange var*!" his guests said, raising their glasses and sipping.

C crossed his legs and said, "Despite your appalling taste in haberdashery, you are looking fit, Alex. Two weeks at your Teakettle Cottage in Bermuda seems to have agreed with you."

"Thank you, sir. But despite my much younger age and condition, I still can't beat this wily sportsman over here at the game of golf."

Trulove chuckled and gazed up at a grand painting of Admiral Lord Nelson's *Victory* at Trafalgar.

"Now, Alex, let me get to the reason I called you both down to London on a Saturday. There's been a bizarre murder in Zurich, according to our chief of station there. A crime that is of great interest, not only to MI6, as you'll soon understand, but to the Crown as well. Spent much time in Switzerland, have you?"

Hawke thought about it. "Well. Let me see. Went to school there briefly, Le Rosey, before transferring to Dartmouth Naval College, sir. Later on, the odd business trips to Zurich, ski holidays in St. Moritz or Gstaad, that sort of thing. Done a bit of mountain climbing there in my younger days, as you may remember. The tragedy on Der Nadel was the beginning of the end of all that foolishness."

"Yes, a tragic event, Alex, tragic. But you did have another go, correct? One more? You almost conquered that mountain a few years ago, as I recall. That's quite a conquest for a semi-professional climber coming out of retirement."

"Thank you, sir. I won't claim it wasn't a bit daunting in the doing. A bit creaky for that sort of thing now. Oh, and I fell."

"Ambrose? How about you?"

"*Mountain climbing?* Me? Good Lord, no!"

"He doesn't even ski," Hawke put in, quite unnecessarily.

"I refer only to Switzerland, Chief Inspector. Spent much time there?"

"Ah. Yes, a good bit, actually. The usual thing. Mostly business in Zurich, but in Geneva and Bern as well. You know the drill, sir. Intricate financial cases involving British clients and old Swiss banks, neither of whom want their names in the papers. Private family matters . . . the odd murder. Investigated a crime involving a lesser-known British royal recently. Lord Emsworth of Blandings Castle, one of Her Majesty's lesser nephews. A kidnapping, just last year. A horse, as a matter of fact, yes."

"Horse?" Trulove said. "Extraordinary!"

"Long story, sir."

"Well. At least you've both been there enough to know your way around. Good contacts, I would say. Knowledge of the history and customs and so on."

"We're going to Switzerland, I take it," Congreve said.

"You are indeed. Something has come up."

Hawke and Ambrose eyed each other across the table. That phrase "Something has come up!" was C-speak for "the poop has hit the poopdeck again."

"Pray tell, Sir David," Congreve said. "What exactly has come up?"

"Well. It won't come as any great surprise for you to learn that the case involves financial misdeeds as well as a grisly murder. The large private bank accounts of a select group in the House of Lords have recently been subjected to very sophisticate hacking attacks. There were substantial losses prior to discovery of the incursion. Not to mention some losses in a number of accounts belonging to Her Royal Highness, the Queen herself."

"The Queen?"

"Yes, the Queen. One of Her Majesty's many charitable accounts in Zurich has been systematically looted over the last six months into near nonexistence. That discovery triggered the investigation. And that, we think, led to the murder of a very prominent Swiss banker.

"And that, gentlemen, is why I asked you here. I hesitate to add that one of the British accounts burgled was held by you, Alex. Your account with Credit Suisse was recently attacked. However, in the main, your cybersecurity bulwarks held fast, Lord Hawke."

"Attacks on my accounts? Really? Hard to believe. I've not heard a word about it from my bankers there."

"Nor will you, except from me. The ongoing criminal investigations are taking place under a blanket of total security so as not to alert the hackers. As of yet, our MI6 lads in Zurich have been unable to trace these attempts back to the primary source. But MI6 Cyber Warfare here in London has been able to verify the origin of one of these attacks as being China. And, more recently, our Russian friends."

"Christ," Hawke said, "here we go again. I've gotten to the point with Putin and the Russians that I much prefer the Chinese."

"I believe we all have, Alex. Behold Putin unchained."

"Hmm. Vlad the Impaler. How did you learn of all this financial skullduggery, sir?" Congreve asked.

"Sheer luck. One of our Zurich station's MI6's techies had his home laptop freeze up while looking at something strange going on. Very strange, indeed. He was simply running a cursory check on the Swiss government's Cybertech Division's UK accounts monitoring that morning when something very disturbing popped up. That was a week ago.

"Our man had somehow tapped into a peek inside the books of all the major Swiss banks with British accounts. He suddenly saw things he'd never seen before. Wild swings in overnight balances. He happened on it while at home, rebuilding his MacBook Air, if you can imagine. He immediately got on to our MI6 station chief in Zurich to alert him to what was going on. And thus the call I received."

"Schultz, was it?"

"Yes. Herr Fritz Schultz. Called 'Blinky' by many of his

MI6 colleagues. Something or other to do with his eyes. He called me late last night. His message was that a prominent banker named Leo Hermann had been found dead by a Swiss Army alpinist near the base of a mountain just south of Zurich. Hermann handled Her Majesty's private accounts at Credit Suisse. Top man. We need to run this thing to ground immediately lest it go any further. And shut down whoever was behind not only the hacking but this very odd murder as well."

Hawke, now fully engaged in the conversation, leaned forward and stared at C.

CHAPTER SIX

"I know Blinky quite well, mostly from alpine climbing together. Do you think this fellow Hermann was involved with the hacking attacks on Her Majesty? Or that he was killed because he was getting close to unmasking the foreign culprits?"

"I have no idea. You both understand that Great Britain itself keeps most of its vast gold reserves throughout Switzerland. But, frankly, Blinky Schultz is far more worried about Her Royal Highness's business than yours, my dear boy. Your name and Hawke Industries just happened to pop up in the mix of attempted hacking."

"Rather surprising, sir; in the world's largest money pond, I'm a very small fish."

"And so I assume this is where Hawke and I enter the picture?" Congreve said, leaning forward. You could almost hear the eager panting as Scotland Yard's famous old dog gnawed at a rather large new bone clenched between his teeth.

"Precisely, Chief Inspector."

"I'm hardly a cyberwarfare sleuth, with all due respect, sir," Ambrose replied. "Don't even know how to tweet."

"*Tweet?* What the hell is that?" C said.

"Some kind of app or other. I have no idea, Sir David."

"An app? What on earth is this man talking about, Alex?"

"Couldn't really say, sir."

"You're a fine criminalist, Ambrose, and no one expects you to tweet or climb anything. But you, Alex, are entirely another kettle of fish. You possess skills that may prove vital to the mission. Hitherto unused in the line of duty, I might add."

"Such as, sir?"

"Mountain climbing, to be exact. I took a look round at all of the available resources in your section. All the CVs, you see. Looking at the various hobbies officers of my own C Section enjoy. No luck at all, until I thought of you. You're simply the only man who meets professional grade qualifications. At any rate, that's why I chose the two of you. The Brain and the Brawn, as it were."

Congreve put his fist to his mouth and coughed discreetly. "I wouldn't mind a bit of climbing. A gentle hill or slope, perhaps."

"No, no, no. None of the brawny bits for you, Chief Inspector. It's that galactic-sized brain of yours that wants exercise now. You'll find these two tangled mysteries worthy of your talents, I assure you. Ever heard of a man called 'the Sorcerer,' either of you?"

"Why no, I haven't," Ambrose said.

"Bit of a mystery, as I say. Very few people have ever laid eyes on him in recent years. And if they did, most are all dead now. Old age or whatever. When he disappeared, he was the most powerful man in Swiss finance. He ruled the roost. And nothing happened or didn't happen in the great Swiss financial institutions that did not have his blessing or his finger-prints on it. You'll both hear a lot more about him from your friend Blinky. Yes, Alex?"

"It's not often I find myself looking into crimes that actu-ally involve both the Queen and me personally. Or have any-thing to do with my own business bank accounts."

"I'll get to all that in due time. Now. Do either of you know anything at all about the *real* Switzerland? By that I mean the inner workings of the country itself. Their military history, for example."

Hawke looked over at Ambrose and said, "No, not really."

"We're all ears, Sir David," Congreve said with all the ea-gerness of a new puppy. "Please, sally forth."

"I don't want to bore you with a lecture."

"Oh, we're never bored," Hawke said brightly, like an overly excited honors student to his Cambridge don.

The old man got his pipe lit and said, "Here you have a tiny nation that has not fought a war in over seven hundred years. And they are fiercely determined to know how to fight one so as not to have to."

"Jolly good!" Hawke smiled. Ambrose guffawed and added, "Marvelous!" which pleased the host no end.

"Switzerland is two times the size of the state of New Jersey, which has, by far, the larger population. Yet there are nearly a million men in the Swiss Army. It's a civilian army, a trained and practiced militia, ready to mobilize instantly. Each citizen serves for thirty years. But all of them, a million of them, mind, are ready to grab their rifles and be present at mobilization points and battle stations all over the country. Within twenty-four hours."

"You have got to be joking," Hawke exclaimed, full of wonder.

"Not even slightly. Most of these citizen troops specialize in combat operations that occur at twelve thousand feet and skyward and—"

"I beg your pardon, Sir David, but is this to be a military operation as well?" Congreve asked.

"Not yet, at any rate, but we must be prepared for the path to lead us in that direction. I cannot say more. But our man Blinky is going to introduce you to someone named Baron Wolfgang von Stuka—or 'Wolfie,' as he likes to be called. Comes from a very long line of aristocratic warriors. Now a highly respected *divisionnaire* in the Swiss Army. Captain, basically. Many call him 'Switzerland's Guardian Angel.' He is the soul of bravery and honesty and a man revered by most of the population, especially the women."

"I look forward to meeting this saint in human form," Hawke said, excitement palpable in his voice. "And finding your murderer for you, sir."

"I'll second that, Sir David," Ambrose said.

"Good. Time to do one's duty," said Hawke, raising his eyes to the magnificent picture of his great hero, Admiral Lord Nelson, as he lay dying on the bloody deck of his flagship *Victory*. The last words he'd spoken were "I thank God that I have done my duty."

Chapter Seven

"All aboard!" shouted the squat little Eurostar porter at London's busy St. Pancras station. Typical London weather, raining buckets and pea soup fog. Hawke and Congreve, each carrying their own luggage, made their way through the hubbub of the crowded platform toward the nearest first-class carriage.

Hawke entered their car first. He dropped his leather carryall on the floor of the freezing vestibule, then turned around to unburden Congreve of his Louis Vuitton hard-sider. The chief inspector was coming up the steps, huffing and puffing as Hawke snatched his suitcase away. Congreve's cheeks had turned bright apple red in the chilly air of the terminal.

"You're a godsend, Alex," he croaked.

"Did you really need to bring this bloody thing? The bag alone must weigh over forty pounds. Are you mad? Ever heard of backpacks?"

Ambrose put one hand against the cold steel bulkhead and paused to catch his breath. Fishing for his handkerchief, he began to mop his brow and said, "Backpacks, you say? No, actually, I have not. What the devil are they?"

"They're what normal people carry things in."

"I did not pack this lovely antique Vuitton suitcase. My wife, who is a woman barely acquainted with normality, did."

Far be it from Hawke to reply to that one. Lady Mars was one of his closest friends, and she had long aided him in his futile quest to keep Congreve out of as much trouble as they could manage. Despite the famous detective's somewhat sedentary lifestyle, he embraced Winston Churchill's famous claim that "There is nothing so exhilarating as to be shot at without effect."

Safe to say Ambrose himself had dodged more than his fair share of bullets during his own legendary career at Scotland Yard. The number of bullets fired at him had decreased somewhat when he'd joined Lord Hawke and his notoriously dangerous lifestyle, but they were still quite numerous.

It was much warmer in the cabin. The two men made their way up the hectic aisle and located their seats. Collapsing into them, they each pulled out a copy of the day's *Times*.

A few minutes later, the train chugged slowly out of St. Pancras Station, heading south out of London, bound for Paris and the Gare du Nord. And thence to Zurich Hauptbahnhof, the central rail station near the beautiful Zürichsee, the banana-shaped blue lake that added so much life to the city.

"Know much about Switzerland?" Ambrose said to Hawke as they crossed the Swiss border some hours later.

Hawke grinned and nodded his head.

Congreve often imitated Sir David's brusque manner, his whisky-seasoned admiral's bark. Hawke laughed.

"Could you believe that?" Hawke said. "Old boy had clearly been hard at his Google all morning long. Just wanted to show off."

They both chuckled, then picked up the books they'd carried along for the train ride. Congreve's was Conan Doyle's *Hound of the Baskervilles*, of course. He proudly announced he was reading it for the twentieth time. He rarely strayed from the tales of his life's epic hero, the incandescent master detective Mr. Sherlock Holmes.

Hawke was thumbing through *The Deep Blue Good-by*, another tale in a brilliant series about his beloved sunburned and sandblasted knight-errant, Travis McGee, Slip F-18, Bahia Mar marina, Fort Lauderdale. What a life! Living on a houseboat, a bachelor in paradise who had his pick of every bikini tan on the beach and— And Ambrose interrupted his reverie.

"You said earlier that you'd climbed Der Nadel once before. 'White Death,' I believe you called it."

"Yes. Rather odd, isn't it? The old man wants me to climb the one mountain in all of Switzerland that I've never conquered. I still have dreams about that wicked bitch all the time."

"I've never heard you speak much about that experience. Tell me more."

"I'm terrified of that hill, frankly. It's just rock, snow, and ice like all the rest. But this bitch almost seems like she *wants* to kill you . . . like you're not anywhere near good enough for her."

"It's that bad?"

"Much worse. There's a reason so many climbers meet death up there. It's insane to even try to cheat it. That's why they come for it. A sheer vertical face called the Murder Wall, smooth as glass. Survive that, and you've got a shot at reaching the summit. Which is a bloody rock spike that forgives nothing. It's like a giant needle scratching at the top of the world."

"Hence the name Der Nadel? The Needle."

"Yes. Vertical faces, treacherous ice fields, swept by appalling wind and ice storms. Barely anything to hold on to or even stick your ax into. Bloody hell thing that monster is, I'll tell you that."

"So why did you do it?"

"Reach the summit, do you mean? Oh, I didn't. I very nearly fell to my death from the north face. Chaps had to come up and bring me down. One of them continued on, reaching the summit looking for another climber who'd gone missing."

"And you're actually willing to have another go? After that nightmare? Isn't that, as you said, 'insanity'?"

"More than willing, Ambrose. Determined."

"Ah. If at first you don't succeed—why on earth would you even dare to—all because your—"

"Because my grandfather's up there."

There was a silence then between the two of them. Hawke abruptly picked up his old Travis McGee paperback again and pretended to read for a while. Then he put it down and stared out his window for a very long time as they began a long climb up into the sunstruck white-tipped Alps. He finally slept a bit, with his chin on his chest.

CHAPTER EIGHT

Zurich

"You can wake up now, Alex, we've arrived in heaven."

"What?"

"Switzerland. You heard me, time to go check into the hotel and have a dram of the Scottish elixir before I expire."

They found a cab and soon were headed up a wide boulevard that hugged the lakefront. Their hotel was a treasure called the Bauer au Lac. It occupied a prime bit of real estate directly overlooking Lake Zurich, with views of the snow-covered southern Alps that stretched away to Italy.

Having both showered and changed into fresh shirts, slacks, and jackets, they met in the hotel bar a little before seven. Hawke arrived first and ordered his favorite Bermuda rum, Gosling's Black Seal.

"You're right," Ambrose said upon arrival, taking the stool adjacent to Hawke. He looked around the paneled room. "This is a rather spectacular old inn. Exquisite antique furnishings and art, even in my little room. Very Belle Epoque. But with a touch of the modern."

"Very what? Very belle . . . something or other."

"It's French."

"I know what bloody language it is! What does it mean?"

"Oh, never mind. Don't get so cranky."

Hawke took another sip of his cocktail and said, "Feel like I'm stepping back in time a century or two every time I stay here. Glad you like it. What are you having?"

Congreve summoned the barman and ordered a tumbler of The Macallan 18, his favorite single malt whisky.

He said, "I was very distressed to hear about your experiences with that cursed mountain, Alex. The White Death. Gives me a shudder just to say it out loud."

"Well, let's just say it's been unkind to my family. But, as I said, if I can find a bit of time after we've tidied up all the loose ends here, I fully intend to give that bloody hill another run for its money."

Ambrose caught a glimpse of Alex's expression and decided not to reply to that.

"Tell me about this chap of yours here in Zurich," Congreve said, glancing at his watch. "Herr Schultz should be arriving any moment. What's the scoop on this fellow, Alex?"

"Our Zurich station chief for the last decade or so, as you already know. Fritz Schultz is an interesting study. Born in Germany and moved to Zurich later in life. Promoted to captain in the German Navy at a very young age. Decorated more than once. C recruited him to join MI6 in the late nineties.

"Blinky has proved himself invaluable in a town that is always chock-full of scoundrels and spies. I've dealt with him many times and found him to be scrupulously honest, brave as an oak, and built like a fireplug—here he comes now. "Hullo, Blinky, it's Hawke, over here!"

The new arrival lit up at the sight of his old friend and hurried toward Hawke with his arms spread wide. He had a very brisk manner and was wearing an old seaman's cap upon his head.

"Hawkeye, how grand to see you again!" Herr Schultz embraced Hawke, patting him warmly on the back, then took the newly vacated stool beside his friend.

Congreve, with his ex-London copper's knack for memorizing faces on sight, thought Herr Schultz looked somewhat as Hawke had described. But, upon closer inspection, Ambrose found the fellow's face to be made up of points and angles and a prominent, bill-like nose, which gave him the look of a woodpecker in a captain's hat. All of this combined with some neurological quirk that caused him to blink rapidly and incessantly. It was this tic, obviously, that had earned him his ship's nickname of Blinky. He was a right wise and jolly old elf, with those busy blue eyes and a shock of white hair on his head, and he was built like a bank vault.

"And you as well, Blinky," Hawke was saying. "Please say hello to my partner in crime, former Chief Inspector of Scotland Yard, Ambrose Congreve."

"Pleasure," Congreve said, extending his hand.

"Pleasure's all mine, sir," Blinky replied.

The three men exchanged more pleasantries and happy chitchat before settling down to the business at hand.

Hawke said, "So, Blinky, let's get down to cases. Could you please give us a quick update? Sir David only provided us with the bare bones of this astounding case."

The man smiled, withdrew a brier pipe from inside his jacket, and got it going before he replied.

"Have either of you ever heard of a man living here in Zurich named Baron Wolfgang von Stuka? 'Stooka,' like the Nazi dive bomber. You will. He's suddenly playing a significant role in this money mystery of ours. One of the most powerful and popular financial men in town. A highly respected Swiss Army officer, as well."

"I have a feeling we're going to be hearing a lot more about him," Congreve said.

CHAPTER NINE

"**B**aron von Stuka," Blinky said, puffing away on his pipe like a steam locomotive, his eyes rapidly fluttering, "is a *divisionnaire* in the Swiss Army. Friends call him 'Wolfie.' I do. A captain, basically, when he's called to active duty in the mountain passes. He's the one man who might help us get to the bottom of this. Not only help to unravel this financial sneak hack attack but to find those responsible for it, take them off the board. So far so good, right? And then a game changer happened.

"He rang me up a week or so ago and said one of his grenadiers, a Lieutenant Hartz, had a very odd thing happen while on search-and-rescue duty that morning. He took a near fatal fall. And then found a decapitated head on the snowy ledge that had broken his fall. Saved his life."

"A what?" Congreve exclaimed.

"A head. Hartz thought it was just a head, lying frozen on the snow. That's what it looked like anyway. He took a squad of grenadiers back up to the site next morning. They dug away all the ice beneath the head for over an hour. And, voila, le corpse! Dressed quite oddly. Baron von Stuka has a strong feeling that, based on its appearance, that body is related to our mystery."

"How?" Hawke asked.

"Wolfie intends to investigate it. There were certain things about the corpse that . . . never mind, I'll let him tell you about it. He's not saying anything for public consumption, but privately he thinks he may well have found the Bat Cave."

"Bat Cave?" Congreve said.

"Hmm. Bat Cave, yes. I'm sure Sir David mentioned someone known as 'the Sorcerer'? When he briefed you?"

Congreve said, "He did. Very mysterious chap, apparently. Disappeared a decade or more ago."

"Wolfie believes Sorcerer may be involved in this computer crime wave. And that the corpse may lead us to the Sorcerer's lair. Where he's been hiding all these years."

"Batman is our new villain? How marvelous!" Congreve said, smiling amiably at Blinky.

"Batman? No, not exactly. No cape, no Robin, no Batmobile. But a cave? Maybe, maybe not. It's something we must talk about after you both know a bit more about the case. Yes?"

Blinky was indeed a delight, Congreve thought. He had an infectious smile, lightning-quick mind, and a very direct approach to things. He wore a lovely Austrian jacket, grey wool with forest-green trim and reindeer-antler buttons. Blinky seemed to epitomize all of Congreve's most cherished romantic notions about the eccentric Swiss character come down from the mountains. And he wanted that grey wool jacket.

Blinky said, "Let me tell you a little about Wolfie, Chief

Inspector: Baron Wolfgang von Stuka. Patriarch of one of our country's wealthiest, oldest, and most noble families. A citizen soldier and a businessman. That is our baron. No matter where this trail leads us, Wolfie will be a vital asset to us, as you'll soon discover."

"Sir David told us only about von Stuka's sense of duty and sterling reputation for bravery," said Hawke. "Now tell us the truth about this fellow who's too good to be true."

Blinky smiled. "Of course, of course! We grew up together, and my children and Herr Baron's children are still great friends. Well. Where to start? It's a little-known fact that Europe's twelve ruling families remain deeply competitive about who has the swankiest palaces, the biggest yacht, the shiniest diamonds, and the biggest bank balances. It's always been an expensive business, being a Royal. Wars to fight, castles to build, daughters to marry off, pageants to perform, and all that.

"Then there is our poor Wolfie. Poverty stricken by the standards of the original Twelve Families. He keeps the von Stuka family dynasty going by selling off land and art. He also invested in a wildly successful business in Texas that develops not oil fields but hybrid rice for developing nations. He has devoted his life to charitable work, much like your friend Prince Charles, Alex.

"These exalted people are expected to look shiny and regal and good on a postcard. But you'll never see a picture of Wolfie published anywhere. He's too modest and too humble. No Rolls in his garage—he drives around Zurich in an old blue Lexus."

"I find this chap rather likable already," Hawke said.

"Hmm. I suspect you two will get along, Alex. Wolfie was recently asked by a newspaper reporter about his legendary humility. His answer? 'I would rather not talk about humility, as to do so would not be humble.' That's Wolfie in a nutshell."

"So when do we finally meet this saint in human form?" said Hawke. A modest man himself, he hated exorbitant praise on anyone.

"Tomorrow morning. He's on maneuvers with his Tenth Mountain Division high up in the mountains south of Lucerne, but he knows you're both coming to talk. I'll provide you with transportation, of course. We'll be driving down there at first light, a little under an hour. And then military transport to his classified location high in the southern Alps.

"Hope you don't mind driving in a fifty-year-old Mercedes 200 with studded tires for the first leg of our journey. Heavy snow tomorrow. Anything else? If not, I'll have a schnapps and then on to a lovely fondue!"

"Splendid!" Ambrose said. "I could eat a horse."

"We have that, too, Chief Inspector. A great delicacy here at the hotel Bauer au Lac!"

Hawke laughed out loud.

"You'll get to see the famous Eiger tomorrow—you know, the one they filmed that spy movie about. Clint Eastwood, I think, yes."

"I've seen that mountain from a distance but never climbed it," Hawke said. "Looked down on the Eiger from near the summit of Der Nadel. Quite a spectacular sight."

"Quite the view from up there, Alex," Blinky said.

"Not really. I was hanging upside down by my heels at the time."

Chapter Ten

The two Englishmen got their first glimpse of Baron von Stuka the next morning as he climbed down from his command vehicle. It was a clear and frosty morning in mid-December, and a giant, bright red Sno-Cat with brilliant white Swiss crosses on the doors was gleaming against the mountain newly frosted with snow. The sun was shining, almost blinding at this altitude, and Hawke had to use his binoculars to see their host.

He strode quickly down the length of a long, wide swath in the snow, one the Sno-Cat had just carved on the slope. It was near a wide crevasse on the snow-packed Eiger, six thousand feet above the lake below.

Hawke raised his binoculars to his eyes and watched von Stuka's descent down the mountain. On the baron's shoulders—and nested in the fleece of his Finnish hat—were pairs of stars. There was a Swiss cross in the center of each star. The *divisionnaire* was tall and trim, with wavy dark hair, a narrow, suntanned face, and a manner about him that was quietly convincing.

It occurred to Hawke that Gregory Peck in his military film roles had resembled the baron, who in turn actually resembled General Douglas MacArthur.

Blinky, his apple-red cheeks wrapped in a fur-trimmed parka, said, "The baron must go to remote locations to see his men in action. In Switzerland there are no Fort Braggs, no Fort Knoxes like the U.S. Army has, you see, no vast terrains set aside for explosive games. If the Tenth is using live ammunition, like today, they must climb to the higher elevations to shoot and blow things up. This company of grenadiers looks upon themselves the way United States Marines or your SAS men see themselves. A breed apart. Only these men specialize in combat that takes place at altitudes of six thousand feet and skyward."

"Most impressive, Blinky," Hawke said, and he honestly was impressed.

"These Tenth Mountain Division troops are all technical climbers, extreme skiers, demolition experts, and crack shots. They sleep on granite mattresses and eat chocolate-covered nails. Some of them, like Wolfie, are wealthy bankers, or CEOs of major Swiss corporations. The older man you spoke to when we first arrived, carrying the heavy machine gun, is the chairman of Nestlé.

"Others are chauffeurs, dental technicians, civil engineers, and alpine guides. One young lieutenant up here works for IBM in Armonk, New York. Today the grenadiers have uncovered an enemy command post and are moving up toward it under the covering live fire of Russian automatic weapons, simulating what might be a reality one day. You see them up there, yes?"

"We do," Congreve said, the binocs glued to his eyes.

"Crawling through snow under bullets, they will soon reach the lower wall of the Russian command post, a dotted line in their minds, and rig it with Semtex explosive charges. You'll soon see the explosion. Chunks of broken rock will rise out of the snow and fly in all directions, right over the heads of our warriors . . . ah, here he is . . . *Guten morgen, Herr Baron!* We made it!"

Wolfie laughed and embraced Schultz, delighted to see his childhood friend again. "So you have, so you have! And these are your two colleagues just arrived from London. *Wilkommen*, both of you! I am Baron von Stuka. A great pleasure to meet you."

"I'm Alex Hawke, Baron," Hawke said, extending his bare hand. "Blinky told me I may call you Wolfie?"

"Please do, Lord Hawke, everyone does. And you are Chief Inspector Congreve, yes? How do you do? I've been looking at you on Wikipedia recently. You're quite famous, you know, Chief Inspector. A highly respected criminalist well known in the newspapers as 'the Demon of Deduction,' the modern Sherlock Holmes! I'm very honored to meet you, sir. We will need a man of your brilliance to solve this mystery, I assure you."

Congreve, thrilled beyond measure at the Holmes compliment, shook the baron's hand and said, "Well, I wouldn't go that far, Wolfie. I have had a few successes, but nothing even remotely to compare with my hero, the incandescent Holmes. But, what a brilliant morning up here. Blinky here was just giving us a briefing on what your Tenth Mountain Division grenadiers are doing up there on the mountain. Fascinating."

"Well, it's what we do, isn't it? Mountain warfare. You see what's happening up there right now?"

"They're about to take out a Russian command post, I believe," Hawke said, holding a pair of Zeiss binoculars to his eyes. "Live fire, isn't it? And Wolfie, please just call me Alex. Don't use the title, never have."

"Quite right, Alex it is. Well, where are we now in our little war story? Ah, yes. Do you see those heavy boulders over there? On the far side of the crevasse, just gone in shadow? My men are crawling through chest-high snow toward them. Any idea what they might be, Alex?"

"Enemy helicopters that have just landed?"

Wolfie smiled. "You've either got a very vivid imagination, or you've played these games yourself, Alex. Good for you."

"A little of both, I guess."

Congreve, struggling to get his pipe lit in the wind, said, "Now what happens, Wolfie? I must say this is jolly good fun for me. Never having been a military man, I've never seen this sort of live-fire thing done before."

"Delighted to have you. It was all Blinky's idea. He knew I was up here on maneuvers and said as long as he was bringing you both up here for lunch, why not come up a little earlier and get a peek at what makes the Swiss Army tick."

"A clock?" Ambrose said, stifling a laugh.

"Quite a good one," Wolfie said, then added, "So, Blinky, as you know, my command trailer is up there in that copse of evergreens. Do you think our guests would enjoy a bit of warmth and getting an overview of the operation from up there?"

Blinky Schultz, stamping his ancient leather boots against

the cold, said, "Good idea, Wolfie. I believe you're having lunch served up there in an hour. Why not?"

"To the Sno-Cat, then!" von Stuka said, marching back up the slope and signaling them to follow in his tracks.

Blinky stomped alongside Alex on the climb up to the red vehicle. He said, "I hope this suits you, Alex. Knowing how we wage war at the top of the world might just come in handy one day."

"Are you kidding? I'm fascinated with Wolfie's tutorial. We can talk about the Sorcerer tonight, after all."

"As you can see, my country is prepared for an invasion at some point in the future."

"Russians?" Hawke asked. "I don't see it. Putin isn't that crazy."

"Hmm," Blinky said. "Let's talk about that tonight over dinner at Der Kronenhalle as well, shall we? The Russians may be involved in this financial chicanery. But military issues? That's an entirely different matter."

"Let's go up!" von Stuka said.

"Bear with me," Baron von Stuka said, clearly grateful for the cozy warmth inside his command trailer. Hawke, Congreve, and Herr Schultz, plus a pair of uniformed military observers with powerful binoculars, were all seated in a row of chairs facing a very large window. They were watching the ballet of battle as it played out high up on the mountainside. Hawke was watching the live-fire exercise up above with laserlike focus. Even Ambrose was beginning to appreciate the gift of knowledge that Wolfie was giving them.

He had been explaining the nuances and intricacies of high-mountain warfare while the four of them had been sipping hot cocoa and eating pastries from Sprüngli, the most famous cafe in Zurich. It was, Congreve mused, a lovely way to spend a morning.

Von Stuka stood up to stretch his back and said, "Those huge boulders we've arranged over there, as you correctly assumed, Alex, represent enemy helicopters that have just landed. Remember that for seven hundred years, Swiss soldiers have been the masters of these mountain passes."

"Sorry, did you say you arranged those boulders?"

"Sure. Indistinguishable from real granite, but they weigh only a tenth of the real thing. Brilliant invention created by scientists at the Ministry of Defense. Made of some synthetic rock called Granite 2. Comes in handy in a lot of situations. Good for camouflaging things up in the mountains, for example."

"Extraordinary," Ambrose said.

"Hmm, yes. Ours was a land where the invaders were at a supreme disadvantage. We knew the mountain terrain down to the square inch, every rock and stream. They hadn't a clue. Centuries ago, we could even win battles with falling rocks. Roll them down the mountain and crush the invaders far below. And then helicopters were invented."

"Changed everything, one would assume," Ambrose said, polishing off a lemon tart.

"Yes. The modern Swiss Army has the 'flying horses,' as we call them, to contend with. We have substituted surface-to-air missiles for loose rocks. Should a swarm of enemy choppers come sweeping through that pass some day, we will be ready and—"

At that moment there came a deafening roar, one that echoed down the towering canyons of stone. Not an avalanche, the noise was loud to the point of pain. The enemy communication outpost had just been obliterated in an epic explosion. Giant chunks of granite had been thrown upward, and they now came tumbling down from the sky. As Alex and his friends watched, the Tenth Mountain Division climbed even higher toward their next objective, ducking and dodging the falling chunks of granite.

Shots rang out then, echoing down the canyons of stone.

Chapter Eleven

It was snowing heavily that evening. Outside the hotel, nearly invisible, snow-laden trolleys trundled along on the wide Bahnhoffstrasse, pausing periodically to collect huddled white clumps of passengers waiting patiently at the stations. The view from the windows of Hawke's suite gave onto the city. The spires and many bridges over the river made the scene a wonder for him.

He took the elevator down and met Congreve in the lobby of their hotel. It was one of the oldest establishments in Zurich, built amid gardens at the edge of the lake, and quite the nicest hotel in town. Blinky had made a reservation for four at a restaurant called Der Kronenhalle.

Hawke looked at his watch, saw that it wasn't yet six o'clock, and suggested they have a quick drink in the cozy hotel bar before adjourning to the restaurant.

"Quite an exciting and informative day," Alex said after they'd ordered from the barman. They'd managed to snag the last two spots left at the heavily carved mahogany bar.

A buoyant hum of conversation was audible over the happy tinkling of ice cubes in crystal glasses. A very civilized Friday night in one of Europe's most beautiful capitals.

"Exhilarating up there, wasn't it?" Ambrose said, casting a glance at an extraordinarily beautiful ash blonde who'd just entered the room and was glancing their way. She was resplendent in a grey-and-red Chanel suit, loops of white pearls around her neck, and hair sculpted into a chignon held by a diamond pin.

"Rather exhilarating in *here*, too," Hawke said, watching her every move through the crowded bar before she found a small table alone in the corner. She found his eyes again, and hers lingered on his a moment too long. Hawke added, "I'm sorry, what did you say, Ambrose?"

"I didn't say anything. I'm speechless. Good heavens, that's a work of art."

"You don't suppose she's staying here, do you? She wasn't wearing the mink on her arm when she came in."

"Oh, come on, Alex. Don't even get started with that foolishness."

"Foolishness? Are you quite mad? I'm a free man, you know. Over twenty-one."

"Drink your drink and mind your own business. Don't embarrass yourself any further. And close your mouth, it's hanging open."

Hawke reluctantly swiveled back to face the long mirrored wall behind the bar and changed the subject. "Let's talk about Wolfie. I find him a bit of a gent, don't you? A bit over the top. But in a good way."

"Looks like we'll be working with him. He grew on me after a while. In a good way, of course. But still something not quite . . . Don't listen to me. I'm being too harsh on him."

"Fancies himself a gentleman warrior of the first stripe."

"Still, we could do a helluva lot worse," Hawke said, "I saw you speaking briefly about one of his men finding the murder victim in the snow. Anything interesting?"

"Very odd, the whole thing is interesting," Congreve Said. "The victim's head was found by a Lieutenant Hartz, one of von Stuka's grenadiers, while he was on the mountain engaged in a search-and-rescue last week. The man thought he'd found a decapitated head, frozen on top of a snowbank at around eight thousand feet. Frozen stiff. Oddly enough, a pair of horn-rimmed eyeglasses were stuck in the snow not a foot from his head! No tracks, no signs of foul play. They finally found a corpse connected to the head and dug it out. Chap seemed to have suddenly appeared there, out of the blue."

"It happens," Hawke said.

"Of course it does. But does *this* happen? The victim was a good looking, well-dressed, mustachioed man in his late forties. At the instant of his high-altitude fall, our doomed alpinist was wearing a three-piece Hardy Amies suit, an Hermes tie, and a pair of Lobb chestnut brogues. Does *that* happen often in the Alps?"

Hawke was astonished. "Impossible. He would have been in mountain gear, the full rig, oxygen, et cetera."

"I quite agree. I've turned it over and over in the nerve center and have come up empty. Anything occur to you? Anything even plausible?"

Hawke paused a moment to consider. "Just one. The victim was thrown out of an open helicopter flying above the Alps."

"Please, spare me. I've already considered that. Do you really think a passenger in an open helo, flying over the highest mountains in the world in the dead of winter, with temperatures hovering around zero degrees centigrade, would have been dressed in a chalk stripe Savile Row suit and wearing a pair of thousand-dollar lace-up brogues from Lobb of Piccadilly?"

"Good point."

"My specialty."

"Fine. You're the murder specialist. So how do *you* think he got there?"

"He just dropped in after a day of shopping in London?"

"Spare me," Hawke said.

"Okay. One, he was killed elsewhere and the corpse was carried up there to a very remote location to be disposed of. Possible, but nonsensical."

"Not even remotely sensical."

"Right. You hire a boat, fit him with a pair of cement shoes, and throw him overboard in the middle of Lake Zurich at midnight."

"And what is your second brilliant possibility?"

"I have no earthly idea. Nor do I think even my hero Holmes would have one. Not this early in the case, at any rate."

"But there's obviously some kind of explanation."

"Of course there is. That's why we're here, dear boy."

"No. That's why *you're* here. You're the brains of the outfit. I'm the intrepid mountain climber, remember."

"Good point, Alex. And what would our intrepid hero surmise, based on the statement you just made?"

"Hell, I don't know, Ambrose. You tell me."

"That mountain climbing will obviously be required to solve this very puzzling mystery."

"She's looking this way again. I think she's extremely lonely. Do you think I might stroll right over there and offer my services?"

"No, I certainly do not. Baron von Stuka and Blinky are waiting for us at the restaurant."

"Be right back," Hawke said over his shoulder.

Chapter Twelve

Hawke, Congreve, and Alex's brand-new friend, the newly minted vice president at Credit Suisse named Sigrid Kissl, were a little late when they arrived at the restaurant. Von Stuka and Blinky were already at the table, on their second vodka martinis.

Der Kronenhalle was the go-to spot in Zurich for both Baron von Stuka and Herr Schultz. In this centuries-old city, few restaurants had more to offer. On the walls hung paintings by Picasso, Chagall, Matisse, Miró, and Klee. It had been a gathering place for artists and poets from all over Europe who'd sought refuge from the Nazis during World War II. And the food was remarkable too.

The baron, resplendent in an exquisitely tailored navy blue blazer and grenadier's regimental tie, got to his feet, smiling broadly, as the newcomers approached the table through a throng of diners.

"Alex! Ambrose! Over here!" he called out.

"Good evening, Wolfie. Blinky," Ambrose said, first to pull out his chair and sit down. "Sorry we're late. I'm afraid

Alex was unavoidably detained at the last minute, and my apologies. Baron, may I introduce Miss Kissl?"

"How do you do, my dear Sigrid?" Wolfie said, offering the exquisitely beautiful woman his hand. "We have met before, I believe?"

"I'm sorry, Baron, you have me at a disadvantage."

"You are Fräulein Sigrid Kissl, I believe. From Credit Suisse. And I am Baron von Stuka."

"Ah, yes, Baron von Stuka," Sigrid said, turning a bit pink. "Of course, now I remember. At the Credit Suisse corporate office. You were having coffee with our chairman last month, were you not?"

"Yes, yes, my dear. We had coffee in the CEO's office. My dear friend Dr. Heinrich Scheel's office, that's right, is it not? He tells me you are his most trusted bank officer."

"Ah, but in fact I was only taking notes for Dr. Scheel that morning, Baron. Still, I'm very pleased that you remember me."

"My dear, you are a very memorable woman in every way, if I may say so."

Hawke, like a warring stag sensing the unexpected heat of battle, was swift to join the fray. "I hadn't noticed that lovely ring you're wearing, Sigrid. Ruby, is it?" he said.

"A red sapphire. Quite rare."

"Stunning. Who gave it to you?"

"Just a friend."

"Ah. Someone who must have strong feelings."

"Oh, he does," she said, glancing across the table.

Hawke maintained his fixed smile.

"Look here, Wolfie, our guests have arrived," Blinky

said, quickly filling the awkward moment. "Let's order more drinks, shall we?"

Hawke took his chair and said, "Sigrid tells me she has been promoted since then, Baron. She's now one of the bank VP's handling some of the U.K. investment portfolios, among others."

"How coincidental," the baron replied, deliberately vague. "Quick, everyone order drinks and take a look the menu. I have an urgent call to take, but I shall be right back. Sigrid, dear, you've met Chief Inspector Congreve, have you not?"

"Oh, yes. We all three met at the hotel just an hour ago."

"Macallan's whisky for me," Ambrose said to the hovering waiter, "and a rum neat for Mr. Hawke. Sigrid, what would you like?"

"A glass of Pinot Gris, please. The Helfrich 2008, if you have it."

When the drinks came, they all raised their glasses, clinked, and said, "Prost!"

"Please don't touch that wine," Congreve said, catching her as she raised the glass to her lips.

"Why not?" she said, alarmed.

"It's turned. Let me order another vintage for you. Sorry. I have a highly attuned and sensitive nose, you see. One of my many weapons. And weaknesses."

While Ambrose summoned the wine steward, Blinky said, "Thank you for joining us, Fräulein Kissl. We were just discussing a topic you may have read about in the *Neue Zürcher Zeitung* last week. The discovery of a corpse at the base of Der Nadel. Yes?"

She sipped her water and replied, "Apparently, he might

have been a banker. One of ours, even. Just office gossip at this point."

Congreve, Hawke, and Schultz stared at each other in astonishment. "Are you joking?" Blinky said. "A banker? We've heard nothing about any *bankers*."

"Well, you wouldn't have. I only learned of this a few hours ago, just before I left my office. Our bank's director of human resources was on our floor, speaking with a group of our senior managers, and I happened to overhear. The director said that one of our senior bank employees had recently traveled to London on holiday and—"

"So sorry to interrupt, Fräulein Kissl," Ambrose said, smiling at Hawke. "Recently traveled to London, had he?"

"Yes."

"I suspected as much. Please go on."

Wolfie looked at his watch and said, "I have an urgent call to make, but I shall be right back."

After he'd left, Sigrid said, "I knew him rather well. His name is Leo Hermann. Quite good-looking, actually. He was supposed to be back at work this morning, she told us . . . but he never showed up. Calls to his apartment went unreturned, as well as calls from his parents, who knew nothing about his whereabouts. They've not heard from him all week, his mother said. Not that it's him, of course, but still."

"Fascinating," Hawke said. "By the way, what was this chap's name again, Sigrid? Leo Hermann, did you say?"

"Yes, Alex, that's it. The police simply said his disappearance was one of a few linked to an ongoing police investigation, nothing more."

The three men remaining at the table looked at each

other, all unsure as to what they should say next. Clearly she had the trust of the baron. But, as lovely as she was, Fräulein Kissl was a long way from being invited into their circle of confidence.

"Let's order," Blinky said. "Try the Wiener schnitzel, it's the best in town here. *Der beste!*"

After they'd ordered and were making idle conversation about the snowstorm while sipping their cocktails, Blinky said, "So, are you and our friend Alex longtime friends, Sigrid?"

"Not exactly. Unless you call half an hour a very long time."

Everyone chuckled and Hawke said, "Funny thing. Sigrid and I just bumped into each other in the Bauer au Lac bar this evening."

"Alex makes friends very easily," Congreve said, taking a sip of his whisky and avoiding Hawke's eyes.

Sigrid said, "So I've learned. And what do you do in Zurich, Herr Schultz?"

"Ah, yes. Well. I run a small office for a U.K. company here in Switzerland. Import-export type of thing. We export our Swiss chocolates and import their English bacon. A high-calorie business, you might say. But very boring."

"And you, Ambrose? Just visiting?"

"Yes, a tourist, actually. I'm retired from police work now, but I occasionally look into crimes that catch my attention. Idle curiosity, you see. Read about the strange death in the *Times of London*, and here I am."

"What fun. Alex won't tell me what he does. When I asked, he told me he was a male model."

"Well, look at him," Ambrose said. "Man candy. He's quite the lad in all the London gossip magazines. Very much the man about town, you see."

"Man candy," Sigrid said. "I love that, Alex! Suits you perfectly, our new man about town."

"He's kidding," Hawke said, trying to smile. "I'm quite harmless once you really get to know me."

"And after that, Alex?" she purred.

Chapter Thirteen

Wolfie returned just as the food arrived, looking troubled as he picked up his napkin and eyed his piping-hot Wiener schnitzel mit Sauerkraut. However, after a bite to eat, he quickly recovered, and the conversation veered around the table. Time flew.

Everyone was simply having fun and happy to be in such a clean and well-lit space with such good history on the walls.

It wasn't until the coffee had been served that Wolfie artfully steered the conversation back to Sigrid's missing banker. He spoke in a low and quiet voice, encouraging the others to do the same. It was, after all, an extremely sensitive matter.

"I find the mystery of the dead banker at the bottom of a mountain quite fascinating, don't you agree, Sigrid?" he said.

"You, too, Baron? This missing mystery man seems all anyone in my department is talking about. I can't believe the bank has kept it out of the papers."

Von Stuka said, "You won't see *this* in the papers. It was one of my Tenth Mountain Division grenadiers who discovered the body, Sigrid. As the *divisionnaire*, I'm of course eager to help the officials find out what really happened."

"Yes," Hawke said. "Sigrid, we were up on the mountain with Wolfie all morning, watching the Tenth Mountain in combat training. The baron pointed out the exact spot where the victim was found. All very mysterious. The chief inspector here thinks he was thrown out of a helicopter. But, of course, he has a very vivid imagination."

"I certainly do *not* think any such thing! I have no idea how he got there. But I am curious about something else. Tell me, Sigrid, you're rapidly becoming a well-connected banker here in Zurich. Have you heard much at all about this alleged hacking scandal? It is my impression that it's raising eyebrows within the Swiss banking system?"

"Certainly I have heard occasional whispers, Chief Inspector. All rumors and innuendo. No one really knows what's going on. Of course, I work in the client service department. If any of this were true, we would have known about it. And become concerned about the security of some of our British clients."

"Why do you say British, Sigrid?" Hawke said.

"Well, that's the rumor at Credit Suisse, isn't it? That hackers might be going after the Queen of England's gold reserves?"

"The Queen, you say. That's interesting, Sigrid," Congreve said, lighting up his pipe and puffing away to get it lit. "And are there any security problems that you know of involving any other British-held accounts?"

"We're not privy to such details at my level. And, even if I were, I would certainly not discuss it. But I've definitely heard water-cooler gossip that somehow the Queen of England is involved. And I very much doubt Prince Philip himself is the hacker."

"Is anyone even capable of doing such a sophisticated invasion?" Congreve said, leaning closer to her and puffing away on his pipe. "Hacking an account of that importance? With that many firewalls? That would be a massive breach of countless defensive measures. The usual suspects? Iranians? Chinese? Russians? Any real suspects so far?"

"Our chief of cybersecurity, Helmut Koller, is a social friend of mine. I can only say that Helmut is having a difficult time keeping a lid on this long enough to find out if any of these attempted attacks are even real. And, if they are, how deep have the attackers gotten? The Swiss Banking Federation Security Division is breathing down Helmut's neck, I can say that much. Not to mention our chairman, Dr. Scheel."

"I'll tell you one thing," Hawke said. "We'd all better pray there's nothing to this. Because if there is, and it's significant, stand back and watch the world banking community crumble to the ground."

"And as the Swiss banks go, so goes the world," Ambrose added.

Wolfie said, "Exactly right, both of you. If Swiss banking security were to be breached and confidence in our system and its defenses was destroyed, it would be the end of all of us, I assure you, Sigrid. Panic, meltdown of international trade would spread around the world. And, most importantly, trust would evaporate overnight. Every significant nation in the world keeps the vast amount of its private wealth here. Hell, eighty percent of the entire world's wealth is right here in Zurich. Such an event would be cataclysmic."

Hawke said, "Do you agree with the baron, Blinky?"

"I'm just grateful our government and the banks are maintaining a heavy cloak of secrecy until someone gets to the bottom of this. Shut these cybercriminals down before the story leaks out to the world at large. But what do I know? I'm in chocolate."

Wolfie said, "Sigrid, we've only just met. But knowing that our mutual friend, your chairman, Heinrich Scheel, has just demonstrated his faith and entrusted you with your promotion to a Vice President. I've just spoken about you with Dr. Scheel. And now I'd like to make a proposal to you. You don't need to answer me now. Take some time to think about it. Will you hear me out?"

"Of course, Baron, I will do that. But may I ask what your involvement is in this case?"

"You may. Heinrich Scheel and I are old friends since childhood. He's worried about what he sees happening inside the Swiss financial community. Deeply concerned. The first thing he wants me to do is identify the man at the bottom of the mountain. He knows that I myself, and the entire Swiss Army, have enormous manpower and technical resources far beyond his own. He has confidentially asked me to look into the murder. That request from Dr. Scheel is, of course, highly classified information, as it involves our national security at the very highest level. Reveal it at your gravest legal peril, my dear."

"I understand. I give you my word, Herr Baron."

"I give you my trust," he replied. "But from now on you have to earn it."

"Thank you, sir."

"Never abuse it, Sigrid. You must believe me on that one. My thought for you is this. It would be most helpful to all of us if, through your CEO, you became our liaison inside the Swiss banking community. You would be expected to report any relevant information you come upon directly to me. Time is of the essence, obviously."

"You mean that, as of now, I'm a spy?"

"Essentially, yes."

"Fine. You say I could be helpful to all of you. What do you mean by all of 'you,' sir?"

"All of us at this table. Blinky and I are friends since schooldays. He is in the import-export trade, but he's also an international forensic accountant. Alex is not a male model. In fact, Lord Hawke and Blinky are colleagues of sorts."

"So, he's Lord Hawke now, is he? It just keeps getting better, does it not?"

Hawke said, "I never use the title, Sigrid. 'Alex' still works."

"Duly noted," she said.

Wolfie said, "And what about our young tourist here? Chief Inspector Congreve, you see, is only partially retired from Scotland Yard. He has been involved in many investigations regarding the Crown and the British Parliament."

"Nice to meet you all again," Sigrid said with a smile.

"And you," Hawke said, with a smile of his own, "again."

Chapter Fourteen

He didn't see her again for a few days.

He told himself he had to stop missing her; they'd only just met, for God's sake. Besides, he was too busy for romance. He and Ambrose spent every waking moment working the case, interviewing bankers and cybersecurity experts—not to mention Walter Heitz, the crusty old detective from the *Stadtspolizei* who was lead investigator on the case of the missing banker, Leo Hermann.

Everyone they knew, it seemed, was involved. Everyone except the one man they really wanted to talk to—the young Swiss Army grenadier who had actually found the body. Unfortunately, he was in St. Moritz at the moment. Wolfie's Tenth Mountain Division had relocated to the mountains there for even more intensive alpine training. Extreme pursuit skiing under fire and X-treme parasail combat tactics.

It was a brilliant morning, the skies shot through with blue; Lake Zurich was peacefully lapping the shore, while the town's rooftops and church spires were cloaked in a brand-new mantle of purest white.

Hawke eased the silver Aston out of late-morning traffic and rolled to a stop in front of the Zurich Opera House to collect his waiting passenger.

"Hop in," he said.

"Where's Ambrose?" Sigrid asked, peering into the car as she climbed inside. Settling into the leather bucket seat, she said, "What in the world have you done with Ambrose, Alex Hawke?"

"He decided it would be too crowded up here for the three of us, so I put him in the back. Fasten your seat belt."

Sigrid craned her head around. "The back? What back?"

"Ah, yes. I put him in the trunk. He's fine."

"What do you mean he's *fine?*"

"I gave him a warm blanket and a thermos full of steaming coffee. It's only a couple of hours to Geneva. He'll be fine, don't worry about him. He can bang on the lid of the trunk if he needs anything. Don't worry about him, he's used to it."

Sigrid punched him in the shoulder, hard. "Do *not* speak to me as if I had a blond brain, Mr. Hawke!"

Hawke smiled at her and engaged first gear. They slipped into light traffic circling around the Opera House. He'd invited Sigrid to join him at a daylong conference in Geneva.

Fritz Schultz was the keynote speaker. Blinky's lecture, "Cybersecurity 2015," was obviously of interest to her, and Hawke had offered to drive her there. They would be driving along Lake Zurich for a while, which was always a scenic delight. Their destination, the Hotel de la Paix, was just outside Geneva, less than two hours away.

"Alex, stop. Where is Ambrose? You told me he was coming with us."

"Actually? He's conferring with the *Stadtspolizei* this morning. Apparently no identification was found on the body, which is interesting in and of itself. Ambrose is looking into the clothing bought in London now. The Savile Row suit he wore, the Lobb shoes. Seeing what purchase records exist."

"Got it, that's all very good. So. What kind of car is this anyway, Alex?"

"Aston Martin," Hawke said, reaching across her to tighten her seat belt. He'd already noticed the pleasing effects of a tight cashmere sweater on her figure; now, her short skirt had ridden high on her tanned thighs. Hawke made a supreme effort to tear his eyes away before he made a fool of himself.

She said, "I don't even like cars. But this one is stunning. Is it new?"

"It's not. 1964, actually. A DB5. A perfect example."

"Ah, a DB5, of course. I knew that."

Sigrid looked at Hawke after a few minutes and said, "Is this really your car, Alex? It looks and smells frightfully expensive. You didn't steal it, did you?"

"I thought about it. But my moral instincts won out and I bought it this morning. From a private owner in Zurich, a fanatic James Bond fan. He has been e-mailing photos of the car for over a year. He let me drive it around the lake this morning, and I finally succumbed."

"He's a James Bond fan? What on earth does that have to do with anything?"

"This is the DB5 used in *Goldfinger*. Still the best one of them all, as far as I'm concerned."

"You're joking. I love that film, one of my favorites. And this is the actual car from that film? Sean Connery's car? This 'Lord' business you're in must pay very well."

"Oh, I get by. But, right, this is the exact one in the movie."

"Seriously? So, I guess that means you can squirt oil on the road to lose the bad guys? Or eject me up into the clouds if I say or do something you find annoying?"

"Depends on what you say, darling, but absolutely. That's why I'm taking this route round the lake. If you do force me to eject you, at least you'll come down into the water after I launch you into space."

She smiled at him. Her mood seemed to be improving with every mile they covered.

"How long a drive, James?" she said, wrinkling her nose at the scent of air redolent with waxed leather and Castrol motor oil.

"As long as it takes, Pussy."

CHAPTER FIFTEEN

H awke was playing country music on the car's 8-track audio system: *Willie Nelson Live at the Opry!* After a bit of small talk, Sigrid had settled deep into her bucket seat and turned her face to the scenery. She was, for many miles, content to watch the seamless parade of Swiss postcard pictures floating past her window.

He watched her out of the corner of his eye. He felt just the way he'd felt that first night—he couldn't take his eyes off her.

He would remember later on that he began to fall in love with her that day. An hour later, they were cruising along the shores of Lac de Genève. Hawke found the scenery breathtaking; the white-capped Alps marching along the shoreline beneath a crystal-blue sky. It was another idyllic Swiss scene you couldn't duplicate anywhere else in the world.

"Getting close," Hawke said for something to say.

"I do love this old car, Alex. It's very cozy. I don't know anything at all about old sports cars, but this one is a dream. Will you be driving it back to England when all this is over, Lord Hawke?"

"Want to come?"

"Down, boy."

"I'm quite serious, you know."

"Precisely what I'm afraid of."

"I was afraid you'd say that."

"Tell me something, Alex, what's your real interest in this murder mystery of ours? I can understand the motives of your two friends, but not yours. You don't seem to fit the profile the way Ambrose and Blinky do. So tell me, why are you really here, your lordship?"

"Good question. I might actually answer it some day."

"Wait. You're really not going to tell me why you're in Switzerland? After we all took that vow of secrecy together?"

"No."

"Because?"

"I don't trust you."

"That's odd. Wolfie does."

"Whatever Wolfie does or does not do is no concern of mine. Tell me something, Sigrid. Do you trust me?"

"About as much as you trust me. Which is to say, not a lot."

"Are you sleeping with Wolfgang von Stuka?"

She gestured classically and said, "What? How dare you! I'd no idea you were so ill mannered!"

"Doesn't matter. Just curious. Calm down or I'll eject you."

"Why would you even say such a thing to me?"

"Wolfie had quite a hard time concealing his heat at dinner that night."

"Don't be absurd. And even if he did, so what?"

"Did he give you that red sapphire ring?"

"No. We just met, Alex, for God's sake. Besides, although he's a very attractive man, he's married. Are you?"

"No."

"Liar. I don't trust you."

"Cheap shot, Sigrid. I said I'm not married and I'm not. I fell in love with a Russian woman in Moscow many, many years ago. We never married. We had a son. He's six years old now. His name is Alexei. He's my whole life now. His mother was arrested for something I'd done in Moscow. She's held captive in a KGB prison in Siberia. I can't get her out. Her name is Anastasia. We both miss her every day."

Sigrid let a long time pass before responding. "For the record, Alex Hawke, you're a very attractive man, too."

Hawke glanced over at her and smiled. "I'd trust you more if you started telling the truth about the damn ring."

"Oh, all right, Alex, just to get you to shut up about it. I kissed him. Once. Nothing more. He invited me to dinner the same day we met in Dr. Scheel's office at the bank. I accepted his invitation. We had a very nice time. He dropped me off at my apartment. He wanted to kiss me at the door, and I let him. The next day this ring appeared on my doorstep. I tried to return it to him next morning, of course, but he adamantly refused it. He's a very attractive man, as I said. Every woman in Zurich is in love with him. What of it?"

"Just curious," he said with a grin.

"Well, now you know. I hope you're happy."

"Very."

Sigrid turned her face to the window, the image of his fleeting smile imprinted on her brain. She thought back to the evening before. She'd just been getting ready for bed. It was after ten when Blinky had called her apartment. He'd had a question about the late Leo Hermann's responsibilities at the bank. Just before she'd hung up, she'd asked him about Hawke, what kind of man he was, what he was really like. When he'd asked her why, she'd replied, "Just curious."

"He's a warrior," he had said, after thinking a moment about her question. "Royal Navy fighter pilot, now just Commander Hawke. He delights in the gamesmanship of war and is said to be utterly ruthless, albeit in an engaging way. You have to understand, Sigrid, he's part Machiavelli, part schoolboy. The Machiavellian side can be cruel, but the schoolboy is always waiting round the corner. And then there's his love of this dangerous game he's playing, that we're all just playing; it just bubbles to the surface; the fun and audacious hazard of it all fills him with infectious delight. Sorry to go on, but he is a bit complicated, you see."

"And those eyes, my God."

"Yes. I don't think I'll ever meet another man like him, Sigrid. And you're right. Such eyes that man has! My Lord, he can look right through you and see the inner workings of your immortal soul while he's talking to you."

She had sighed and hung up the telephone. And, later, she'd turned out the lights, taken to her bed, and slipped into her dreams. And she had taken him with her.

Chapter Sixteen

Hawke downshifted, caught second gear, and accelerated into a tight curve, the Aston's powerful 6-cylinder motor howling, the Dunlop tires chirping as he came tearing out of the turn. They actually *were* running a bit late, but then, that was just an excuse. He could now see the hotel in the distance, perched beside the lake.

They met Blinky in the Hotel de la Paix restaurant soon after his speech in the ornate gilded ballroom. Hawke found them a table in the sun-filled dining room paneled in old walnut, with tall windows overlooking the frozen shores of Lake Geneva. Full of lively chatter, clinking glasses, and busy waiters.

Hawke picked up his menu and said, "Well done, Blinky. Most, if not all, of it was way over my head. But I'm sure Sigrid learned quite a lot. She spent the entire time taking notes, for God's sake. And I didn't realize you were quite so funny in public. You should be doing stand-up comedy instead of pushing chocolate on the unwary British."

Blinky blinked his eyes rapidly and laughed. "I have only

one rule in public speaking. Don't bore the audience. Even if it's about something as excruciatingly boring as cybersecurity. God. I got tired of listening to myself."

Sigrid laughed. "I wasn't going to say it, but I usually find PowerPoint presentations uniformly stultifying. Yours was very funny, Blinky."

The waiter arrived with their three Bloody Marys, and Hawke said, "You said you had a bit of news for us when you rang last night, Blinky. Don't be shy about sharing it."

"Hmm. There are developments. Firstly, Wolfie finds himself snowed under at St. Moritz. His Tenth Mountain is immobilized, and he himself has moved down to Badrutt's Palace in town. He'd like us to drive over, and he's booked three rooms for us at the Palace."

"When?" Hawke said.

"Tomorrow being Saturday, he thought you could make it, Sigrid. We'll meet him at noon if that works for you both?"

"Absolutely," Sigrid said.

"Good, that's done. Let me tell you more about our frozen corpse, if I may, and where he might actually have come from."

"Please do."

"I had a little chat with Wolfie's young grenadier yesterday," Blinky said, "the one who discovered the body. The soldier's name is Lieutenant Christian Hartz, from Bern. He was excused from duty in St. Moritz yesterday in order to show me the exact spot where he'd found the body. Veddy interesting, veddy, veddy interesting."

"Just tell us, Blinky. Don't be a dramatic Nazi about it. You're not on stage anymore."

Blinky laughed at himself. "It's dramatic enough, I assure

you," he said. "Do you remember that when you and Ambrose first arrived in Switzerland, I mentioned something about the Bat Cave and the Sorcerer?"

"Of course. Batman. We've been curious about that ever since," Sigrid said. "What is the connection, Blinky?"

"As you, darling Sigrid, are well aware, the Sorcerer disappeared from sight about ten years ago. The most powerful man in Switzerland simply vanished into thin air. In the papers for months. There was the inevitable nationwide search, Interpol was involved, but in the end they came up empty. Even in his seventies, the Sorcerer was a strong mountaineer. Climbing was his passion. It was finally decided that he had been solo up on a mountain and fallen to his death. The body was never recovered, adding to the shroud of mystery."

"The BBC did a documentary on his disappearance many years ago. Remember, Blinky?" Sigrid said. "Perhaps we could get a copy for Alex?"

"Great minds think alike, and so do ours," he said, pulling a DVD out of his jacket pocket and handing it to Alex.

"Fascinating. I'll watch it tonight."

"Tell us about the Batman connection," Sigrid said. "We're all mystified."

He blinked rapidly and said, "Ah, yes, the mythical Bat Cave. Well, our notion is entirely theoretical. But one of the more interesting theories is this. It was advanced early in the police investigation of the death. That is, that the Sorcerer may be hiding in one of the thousands of abandoned air force bases that still exist all over Switzerland. Like that of the Seventh Fighter Squadron of the *Schweizer Luftwaffe*. With its advanced F/A-18s and—"

"Hold on a tick, Blinky," Hawke said. "Abandoned air force bases? How the hell does anyone hide at an abandoned air base?"

"I assumed you'd ask that question, Alex. I'm now about to reveal a state secret, so treat it as such. We never talk about these things. Ever since our *Luftwaffe* was founded in 1914. Since our country is so small, its size creates a military problem. Our military has much to hide. That's why you see tiny hidden airstrips, like Band-Aids, all over the countryside.

"What you do *not* see are the hangars themselves or the explosives rigged beneath all the bridges on our borders. Or the massive heavy artillery hidden in place to prevent an invading enemy from clearing or repairing the damage from a blown bridge. The Porcupine Principle applies not only to all of our bridges but also to all highways and railroads.

"Concealed explosives, heavy guns, and artillery all around you number in the tens of thousands. And even that number is deliberately understated. You might double or triple it for our purposes. Mountains everywhere have been made so porous that entire Swiss Army divisions are based inside them. Even as we speak there is one not five miles away."

"You're joking," Sigrid said.

"Oh, but I'm not. There are weapons and soldiers under barns. There are countless long-range cannons inside pretty houses. Where Swiss highways run on narrow ground between the edges of two lakes, like the highway you just took, or run at the bottoms of cliffs, man-made rock slides high above the roads are ready to slide. We still throw rocks at the enemy, you see. Voila—the Porcupine Principle."

"Which is what, exactly?" Sigrid asked.

Blinky smiled and said, "You even *think* about pricking us, we prick you back. And we prick you exponentially harder than you can even conceive. It's why we've never endured wars or occupations in over seven hundred years."

Hawke smiled. "They all know you're bad, Blinky, they just have no bloody clue just how bad you are."

"Precisely," he said. "And believe me, we are far, far badder than I've led you both to believe. Our forces spend twelve months of every year learning how not to go to war. Sorry, what were you saying, Alex?"

"Tell us more about these *Luftwaffe* bases hidden inside the Alps. The ones where our mysterious Sorcerer may have been hiding in plain sight for lo these many years."

"Of course. Our F/A-18 fighter bases, too, are all hidden in plain sight. That is to say, *Schweizer Luftwaffe* squadrons and attack helicopters reside within hangar complexes constructed deep inside hollowed-out mountains, from one end of the country to the other. Obviously, in order to shield them from enemy air attacks."

"Obviously," Hawke smiled. He was a bit incredulous about Blinky's revelation, having never been made aware of Switzerland's secret fortifications and hidden air force before. That information was clearly one of the country's most closely guarded secrets.

Sigrid said, "This is astounding. How in the world do they get the jets out of the hangar and up into the sky?"

"Simple. Airplanes and choppers are brought up from the vast underground hangar facilities by a system of high-speed elevators. And then launched by catapults, exactly like those found on modern aircraft carriers."

"Launched how, exactly?" Hawke asked.

"The peaks of countless numbers of our Alps contain runways hidden behind extraordinarily realistic granite-plastic blocks. They are, in effect, movable sections of fake rock. Hydraulically controlled. Virtually undetectable. Climbers make their way up to the summits every day without any idea of what lies inside the face of the mountain they're on. In case of attack, all of these false sections withdraw hydraulically inside the mountain, creating airfield runways in the sky. Our commanding officers are so good, we can now get an entire squadron airborne in twelve minutes."

"Good God," Hawke said. "Astounding."

CHAPTER SEVENTEEN

"So what you're saying is that it's entirely possible that Sorcerer is living somewhere inside a mountain?"

"More than possible. If he's still alive, that's where Wolfie and I believe we'll find him."

Hawke was scratching his day-old casual Friday stubble. "And thus the focus on Leo Hermann, the man in the three-piece Savile Row suit who fell off the top of a mountain and lost his head."

"Yes, Alex, that is correct. As you know, Hermann was discovered near the range of mountains where records indicate the honeycombs were sealed with cement in the 1930s."

"Yes. He was found on a ledge halfway up Der Nadel, was he not?" Hawke said.

"All the more reason to zero in on that particular mountain."

"Any hard evidence that your suppositions are correct?"

"Yes. Ambrose called me early this morning from *Stadtspolizei* HQ. The official police forensic autopsy indicates injuries consistent with a fall of roughly six feet into a snowbank. Almost directly below the Murder Wall."

Hawke asked, "Why not inspect the Wall using helicopters? Find the hidden entrances somewhere on the face?"

"Good thinking. In fact, it was Wolfie's first thought. We discussed that idea at length but came to the inescapable conclusion that the idea was not feasible. The sound of hovering choppers outside would alert anyone inside. Steel doors would instantly seal the mountain for good. Instantly impenetrable. Impervious to any attack by air, leaving us no choice but to use heavy artillery to blow a hole in the side of our nation's most infamous tourist attraction."

"I see your point," Hawke said, mulling it over.

"You don't seem very happy about the prospect of scaling the Murder Wall, Alex. Frankly, no one in his right mind could fault you if you decide not to attempt it again. I, for one, would never blame you. You came extremely close to dying up there."

"No, no," Hawke said impatiently, "that's not what I'm thinking about at all."

"Then what *are* you thinking about, Alex?" Sigrid said, her eyes suddenly clouded with fear.

"Blinky, get Wolfie on your mobile right away. Tell him we won't be coming to St. Moritz. Tell him something rather more pressing has come up."

"You're going up there, aren't you?" Sigrid said, her voice trembling.

But Alex never replied.

He was quietly staring at a soaring white peak far in the

distance. It stood there, towering over the others surrounding
it and putting them all to shame.

The following two weeks flew by with near miraculous
speed, he noticed. He spent long days in mental and physical
preparation for his imminent ascent. Two frostbiting days in
the mountains, three exhausting days in a stifling-hot Tenth
Mountain classroom, studying his evolving route of attack.
Wolfie's ranking army alpine experts were merciless to the
point of sadism.

They pounded him on everything from projected weather
and storm conditions during his ascent to potential avalanche
and rock fall danger, to his meds and supplements, his pain
tolerance, and his mental stamina.

And, finally, coaching him through a deep-dive investigation into the most recent decade's history of fatal attempts by
climbers seeking to put the notorious White Death on the
proper side of their ledgers.

In the late afternoons, while the great criminalist Congreve was working the murder case and the missing Sorcerer,
Alex and Wolfie went shopping. Browsing the various alpine
gear shops of Zurich, they were like two women trying on
dresses at Harrods, though style and glamour were hardly
their goal. Wolfie wanted to make sure Hawke was well-
equipped before his ascent.

Their only objective was Hawke's ultimate survival in the
coming test of endurance, skill, and luck. Some of his most
basic equipment came courtesy of the Swiss Army. But the
more sophisticated gear, the highly sophisticated, state-of-

the-art climbing equipment and the most advanced survival tools and climbing techniques, all came from a little-known, back-alley shop called Schussboom.

It was very convenient, located off a back street just two blocks from his rooms at the Bauer au Lac. There he met the owner, an elderly man named Luc Bresson, a famous French climber who was both the first and the last man to conquer White Death. M. Bresson was of medium height, bone thin except for his wiry musculature, and exceedingly charming. Blue eyes a'twinkle, a luxuriant white moustache. And laughably bushy white eyebrows sprouting sprigs of hair that looked like the weird antennae of a praying mantis waving about in the breeze.

Bresson's own story was quite amazing. And when Luc heard Hawke's tale of his grandfather's bones and his own doomed attempt to retrieve them, the two men had become fast friends almost instantly. Hawke learned far more in a concentrated half hour with Luc than he had in all the many hours he'd spent in Wolfie's classroom. In two short days, it seemed that Luc Bresson had become both his mentor and his guardian angel.

It would prove to be one of fate's better ideas before all this Sturm und Drang was over.

Hawke spent the better part of that warm, sunny Sunday afternoon in mid-December on the deck of a famous restaurant, high in the Alps. A glorious spot, accessible only by cable car. He and Sigrid had invited Blinky to join them in an alpine brunch at Grossescheidegg, a popular five-star restaurant and *Gasthaus* pitched on the side of a towering mountain.

Hawke stood waiting in the sun on the busy deck, waiting to be shown to their table right next to the rail. He stood transfixed at the sight of the beckoning giant. And he finally came to a startling realization. In truth, he was afraid of that mountain. Even now, seated with his friends at a table on the rail, looking up at the mist-enshrouded pinnacle, his groin tingled with icy fear.

And, yet, still his hands itched for the touch of the bitch's cold and ragged rock, the looming vertical face before him. He felt exhilarated at just the thought of trying to beat the savage into submission once more. Once again, he found himself eavesdropping on that perverse internal dialog, the duel between his flinching mind and his boisterous spirit; a conversation that every serious mountaineer knew so well.

Grossescheidegg was known for its outstanding *Ungarische Goulasch*. The broad terrace, filled with round white metal tables and giant red umbrellas, had spectacular views of the murderous mountain that, even now, beckoned to him. To reach the celebrated watering hole, you had to drive along the lake south of Zurich for roughly an hour. In the center of the tiny village of Verblen was a cable car station. The views from the swinging car alone were worth the trip up to Grossescheidegg, situated at 13,000 feet.

While waiting for their food to arrive, Hawke admired Sigrid standing at the rail among a small group of Italians. She was the long-legged blonde, the one with the deep bronze tan, the one who was using one of the six coin-operated telescopes. The scope she'd deliberately chosen was in a direct line between Hawke and the mountain peak.

The weather had changed drastically over the weekend. Days were now warm and sunny, and Sigrid's wardrobe had been adjusted accordingly.

She had chosen to wear tight white shorts, and very clunky clogs. She bent over the instrument, directing her excellent bottom toward him. He could not help noticing that her splendid mountain tan must have been acquired in those very shorts. Since the advent of very short skirts, Swiss women had returned to those remarkable clogs. Some Bernese wag had once said that Swiss women's shoes had been made by fastidious Bernese shoemakers who had had the shoes carefully described to them on the telephone but had never actually seen them firsthand.

"Quite a spectacular vision," Blinky said, sipping his pale Pinot Grigio.

"I could not possibly agree more," Hawke said, taking a deep draught of his St. Pauli Girl, chosen because the beer label had a bosomy milkmaid in a revealing dirndl. "Simply awe-inspiring," Alex replied, his eyes fixed on this woman who had taken such a hold of his life.

"Alex, my old friend. I refer to the mountain."

"Ah. That, too!"

Alex now followed the direct line created by following Sigrid's telescope angled up to the mountaintop, and focused his eyes once more on what he now thought of as his personal demon.

Chapter Eighteen

White Death. Appropriate name, Hawke thought. Early mountaineers had given the mountains far more benign names: Jungfrau, the Virgin. Monch, the Monk, and so forth. But this particular massif had a far more malicious moniker: the White Death.

Always known to Hawke as "the Bitch."

That was because the alpine pioneers had long ago listed it as one of the "impossible" faces, in the days when sportsmen had engaged in pure climbing, before men had armed themselves with piton and snap ring. Later, many of the "impossible faces" would fall to the record books. But the southern face of his mountain had retained her virginity for a very long time.

Luc Bresson had told him the story. In the mid-1930s, he'd said, the Nazi mountain-and-cloud cult sent wave after wave of fair-haired German youth to have a go at Der Nadel—restless Hitler Youth fueled by a lust to chalk up one more victory on the *Vaterland* side of the scoreboard. Hitler himself offered a gold medal struck with a diamond swastika for the first to make it to the top. Years went by, and, in a neatly regimented sequence, all those flaxen-haired romantics would plummet to their deaths. But the Bitch, in all her glory, still retained her hymen.

A few minutes later, when Sigrid returned to the table, Blinky smiled and said, "Alex and I have just been enjoying the spectacular view, my good woman."

"Disturbing view is more like it," she said. "May we switch places, dear Blinky? I don't think I could stand to sit here looking at that damn thing while I eat."

"Of course you can," he said, and got to his feet to effect the swap. Now seated next to Sigrid, Hawke took her hand beneath the table. It was a private sign between them. He would squeeze it thrice and she would return the favor. Three squeezes meant *I . . . love . . . you!*

"Are you quite all right, darling?" he whispered to her.

"Of course. Don't be silly. Why shouldn't I be? It's just that I don't do very well at this altitude."

But Hawke was no longer listening.

He had turned sideways in his chair. Blinky saw that he was staring up at the needle-shaped pinnacle of Der Nadel. And he had a very strange look on his face. A chill went up Blinky's spine—that look was a cloud of fear, and it was the very first time Blinky had ever seen it pass across Alex Hawke's face.

The jolly threesome spent another half hour or so enjoying the Hungarian soup and the ice-cold Hofbrau beer. Blinky worked his magic, steering the group away from what was clearly the elephant at the table: the bloody mountain that would not leave any of them alone. For his part, Blinky was enjoying the sight of Lord Alexander Hawke flirting with a woman he so obviously had come to care for deeply. And, equally obviously, passionately.

"Will you excuse me for a moment?" Alex said, rising from the table while staring up at his mountain. "Brief change in the weather. A brief moment where you can actually see that infamous needle scratching at the underside of heaven. Have a look. That perpetual mist hanging around the summit is giving me a brief window to . . . I'll be right back."

Sigrid and Blinky sat watching him move through the tourists to the rail, where he fed some coins into the telescope.

"Excuse me," Hawke said to a blond woman dressed in that '70s all-white disco glitz of the long-gone jet-setters. "Would you mind very much moving a few feet to your right? Terribly sorry."

She whirled around as if to say something nasty, got a look at who she was talking to, and said, "Of course not, honey-chile, is this all right? Maybe another foot?"

Hawke nodded, gave her a smile, and stared up at the other bitch there that day. The Murder Wall had disappeared into the mists again. The air seemed to be turning cooler . . . as the mountain was again lost to him. He closed his eyes and felt the warm sun on his face.

The warmth of the weightless mountain sunlight was snatched away time and again by invading wisps of cool high-lands air. He'd lost his precious moment of unfettered observation.

Every time he looked up at the death-shrouded colossus,

he could almost feel it throwing its weight around, almost like it was trying to stare him down.

He felt a chill breeze on his cheek and shivered involuntarily. He flashed on his first attempt at the Wall, how he and his grandfather had been beaten senseless by brutal flash storms from the north, collected and amplified in the natural amphitheater of the Murder Wall. Raging fits of wind and snow that had lashed at them and ripped their goggles from their eyes. These had been the shrieking storms that could instantly snap a man's neck against that sheer rock face. And then leave him to hang there on the face, twisting in the wind, frozen, for as many years as it took for someone to recover him. . . . That had been his thought when his piton had given way and he'd plummeted nearly a thousand feet before jolting to a stop when his line had snapped tight.

The violence of the sudden arrest had broken his left leg. His seventy-year-old grandfather had quickly rappelled down to his position and splinted the fracture. Hawke had insisted he was all right and could wait for the rangers to get him down. After a fruitless argument with his stubborn grandson, the older man had continued his climb to the summit. He had one more mountain to climb, he had always told his friend, one more mountain to climb.

And that was the last they had ever seen of the man who had been his beloved guardian since he was seven years old.

Chapter Nineteen

Blinky watched Alex at the rail for a few moments, then turned his attention to Sigrid while he had the chance.

"You're afraid, aren't you?" he said to her.

"Afraid? Hell, I'm terrified. I care for him, you know. A lot. Aren't you?"

"Not terrified, no. Concerned, perhaps. And then only because I love him."

"I care for him a lot, you know."

"I can see that every time you're together. Do you think you've fallen in love with him?"

"It sounds ridiculous, but I do. We've only been together six days, but our orbits are colliding and it feels like gravity is pulling our souls toward each other. We laugh about it all the time, falling in love so quickly. So, yes, I am terrified. It took me a lifetime to find a real man, a man I could love, and now he wants to kill himself."

"Trust me, he's the least suicidal man you'll ever meet. Alex loves life too much to ever think of ending it."

"So why the hell is he doing this?"

"Two reasons. First, duty. He's vowed to protect his Queen and country, and he'll damn well do it. And, second, a more personal reason. His grandfather is waiting for him up there at the top of Der Nadel."

"What? He said something about that, but I didn't understand it."

"The old man's bones are resting up there. Climbing has long been a Hawke family passion. Before his death, the earl was one of the most celebrated mountaineers in Europe. Alex tried once to return his remains to a shady little plot in Oxfordshire, but he himself had never made it to the summit."

"And now he's trying again?"

"Yes. As well as helping Wolfie solve the mystery surrounding Sorcerer."

"Tell me the truth, Blinky. Does Alex have even a remote idea of what he's doing up there?"

"Yes. He does."

"And why would that be?"

"Sigrid, please understand this. You've been with him a very short time. You're now seeing a side of Alex you have not seen. I've known him forever, and I've seen it all. I know what he's capable of, believe me. And that is anything he sets his mind on doing, frankly."

"You really think he'll survive? Make it up there and back in one piece?"

"I certainly do."

"Tell me why, Blinky. I need to know why you're not terrified the way I am."

"Very well. Alex first visited Switzerland in his early twenties with his grandfather. The Earl wished to see Der

Nadel. He wanted a firsthand look at what he would be up against. Someone should have stopped the old gent. Alex made the first half of the climb alongside him. At around twelve thousand feet, a piton failed, and Alex was hurt. Too badly to continue, but not so bad as to be unable to return back to the base camp.

"His grandfather made his way down to his grandson at great possible risk to himself. He finally reached him in the midst of a sudden snowstorm and got his leg splinted. He made ready to haul him back down to camp. He insisted, but Alex flatly refused his help. He urged his grandfather to keep going. The old man was so close to victory then and—"

"Oh my God. So that's it. Alex feels responsible for his grandfather's death."

"I'm afraid he does. Always has. Very sad, heartbreaking really, after losing both parents at such a tender age."

"But he kept at it."

"He was still in his early twenties. By age twenty-four he had conquered two of the most feared summits in the world, Everest and the Eiger."

"So, he was good, wasn't he?"

"Beyond good. Read the history of that era in the sport."

"Why was he? So good up there in the clouds, I mean."

"My dear. In this rarefied world, there are two types of athletes who choose to climb mountains. First, there is the kind of man who is particularly suited to rock work where the minute tactics of leverage and purchase fit his intellectual style. These men are given the nickname 'Rapier.' They strike, parry, and thrust with speed and precision, practically swinging across the face of the mountain, like Tarzan through the trees; in a kind of zone, with very little contact with the rock itself. They want as little to do with the mountain as possible."

"That sounds like it must be beautiful to watch," Sigrid said.

"Oh, it is. And then there is another man, let's call him the 'Mace.' He wants to batter the mountain into submission with his bare hands, to simply overpower it as he climbs upward. And then, when he is on the ice and the treacherous snow, he pants and bulls his way through waist-high drifts, breasting a path upward like an inexorable engine of fate."

"Fascinating, Blinky. And which type is Alex?"

"Both. He focuses on victory first and foremost, but he loves every step of the way up. It's a joy, because he's made the climb in his mind a hundred times before. Now he is living it and—hello, Alex!"

Hawke pulled out his chair and said, "You two weren't talking about me, were you?"

"Why the hell would we do that, Alex? Blinky was just telling me about how easily men who are newly in love can be made to do what they're told. It was fascinating."

Hawke took a sip of his beer and said, "It's looking quite pleasant up there at the top. Changing weather patterns, a warm front on the way. Push the cold one out of the way. It's time for me to get serious."

Sigrid placed her hand on top of his and said, "Surely you're not going now?"

Hawke smiled. "Oh, no. There's a tremendous amount of work to be done before that. Luc Bresson has arranged a small base camp for us up at the fifteen-thousand-foot elevation. It's called the 'Bivouac.' He's going up with me. Get me

accustomed to the altitude. Do some down-and-dirty practice runs. He says he's going to psyche me up until I'm ready
to shoot up that bitch like a high-velocity projectile."

"When will you two go up?" Blinky asked.

"One week from today. At dawn."

"That gives us a whole week together before you leave,"
Sigrid said. "Let's make the best of it, Alex, can we? You will
be back by Christmas Eve, won't you?"

"Of course I will. And you have no idea what a time we'll
have!" he replied, smiling at her.

And what a time he hoped they would have.

CHAPTER TWENTY

While Alex Hawke was high on an ice field atop some Alp, breathing all that heroic and rarefied air (and hopefully not getting himself killed), Ambrose and Sigrid found ways to keep themselves from thinking about him. It hadn't happened by chance. To no one's surprise, Ambrose had a finger in that pie.

He had arranged a secret supper alone with Blinky. A quiet corner table at Der Kronenhalle on the night before Alex and Luc went up to the base camp. The two conspirators both agreed that Sigrid was slipping into a rather fragile state, consumed with fear and worry for her lover's safety. Blinky believed that the only solution was to find a way to bring smiles to her face. To not let her find time to worry.

"And how do you propose to do that?" Ambrose asked him over brandy and coffee.

"I don't, my friend. I propose that you do it. When she fell in love with him, she got you in the bargain. And I must say she was lucky on both counts."

"She's very glamourous and gay. You don't think she'd be

frightfully bored hanging around with a stuffy old Scotland Yard man twice her age?"

"I do not."

"Well, then, I suppose I've had far less attractive assignments, haven't I?"

Zurich's new odd couple were soon spending their evenings hobnobbing around town. In the evening, they hit the high and low alike, the opera, restaurants, bars, and smoky nightclubs. They danced, drank, and sang karaoke till dawn some nights. And, on the cold, blustery nights, they curled up by a fire with pizza and *The Philadelphia Story* or *Brief Encounter*, two of Sigrid's favorite black-and-white films.

Ambrose had just one rule: he would not leave her apartment until he saw a happy smile on her face and she kissed his cheek good-night.

Mornings were spent working the case. Baron von Stuka had privately told Sigrid that they desperately needed a break; they were fast running out of time as the Sorcerer mounted more virulent attacks. Attacks were up dramatically, so she and the chief inspector redoubled their efforts, running down every possible lead they found.

And then things started breaking in their favor. That afternoon, Sigrid came up with a name. And the next morning, they found themselves on the trail of the killer. They were walking in a section known as the Altstadt, Zurich's oldest medieval neighborhood. Zurich had its own version of Chinatown, called Suddchina. The pea-soup fog was even thicker in these winding streets, swirling in dense clouds up every street and around every corner. The two trench-coated investigators were trudging slowly up street after street, getting confused by the street names. Finally, they found the winding cobblestone street they'd been looking for, a steep incline that was becoming more and more of a narrow back alley to nowhere.

It was hard work gaining traction, or even staying on one's feet on the worn, wet stones. Melting, slushy black rainwater from the top of the hill kept pouring down the steep incline, swirling around their ankles. The fact that it was hard to see beyond their noses didn't help either. Only the pale yellow lights from the up here in Chinatown.

"Now I think we're really lost," Sigrid said, smiling. This was her first taste of real detective work and she found it thrilling. "Let's stop and get our bearings, shall we?"

They paused beneath a dim streetlamp at the mouth of a dark land, partially protected by an awning from the rain. Sigrid shook the moisture out of her frizzy hair. "What's that address again?" she said. She was digging around in her handbag for the map he'd given her.

"What?" Ambrose said.

He was staring in disbelief at his ruined shoes; they were his favorite, and he'd been squishing dirty water with every step up the cobblestones. "Pity to ruin a pair of good brogues," he told her sadly.

"Inspector, this is serious business. Pay attention. We're on a case, remember? Where is that map?"

He reached into the pocket of his coat and said, "Here it is, what's left of it."

She studied the torn and soggy hotel map under the dim orange light from the lamppost as they huddled together, trying to make sense of the thing.

They were looking for the shop of some chap Sigrid had tipped Ambrose to in a midnight call last night.

The night before, the telephone in Congreve's hotel room had rung shortly after midnight. He'd looked at his watch, cursed, and rolled over to answer the damn thing.

"Hello? Whom shall I say is calling?" He always answered the phone like that late at night. A lifelong habit that had stood him in good stead.

"It's me!"

"I don't know anyone named 'me.' Good-night . . ."

"Wait! I've got something!" Sigrid had said as he'd been hanging up. "Just had a call from my friend, Jon Levin, head of the bank's cryptology section here in Zurich. Jon says they're cranking it all night up there. You won't believe what they've stumbled upon!"

Ambrose, hearing the breathless excitement in her voice, had held the receiver to his paisley robe and taken three deep breaths. He'd known this could finally be the break they'd all been waiting for.

"All right. Calm down, Sigrid. Speak slowly and tell me what you've got," Ambrose had said with the inflection favored by Job and the Dalai Lama.

"Okay, Chief, here's what I know so far. One hour ago, diving deep into the deepness, Jon came up with a game changer. He found the e-mail address of a formerly high-level forensic accountant, someone he used to work with in Beijing. The two of them worked together as forensic accountants at Credit Suisse before they both moved to Zurich four years ago. Jon got the top job, and now his former boss was working for him. Apparently, he was not a very good loser. Sounds like a motive, sir."

"This is good. Have you got a name?"

"Sure do. His name is Ding Wong. He left the bank a year or two later under a dark cloud of suspicion. There were some serious 'errors' under his watch. Gold, cash, and securities, all in large amounts, had suddenly gone missing."

"Was this man ever charged?"

"Negative. A *Stadtspolizei* investigation of Ding Wong's online client ledgers revealed suspicious serial hacking from the outside, but nothing the cops could pin on him. Nor could the bank's own chief of cybersecurity, my friend Jon, nail him for it."

Sigrid had said she had admitted during the investigation that she had always found Ding to be hypersecretive and thoroughly unpleasant, two traits she'd always associated with a man who had something to hide. She'd told Jon back then that she still thought the guy was guilty. So what? he'd said. And he'd been right; there had been nothing he could do about it. Until now. Now they were in search of an address at No. 11, Vierstrasse.

The two of them kept prowling the streets, up and down the Vierstrasse, looking for a shop named Military Curios. The rain had turned to sleet, and neither of them had eaten breakfast. Ambrose already had his mobile out and was trying to find an Uber car roving somewhere in this unlikeliest of Uber neighborhoods.

"Good luck," Sigrid told him cheerfully. She kept walking up the hill, peering into one grungy shop after another. The street was chockablock with curio shops, tiny noodle houses, laundries, magic shops, and homeopathic medicine purveyors.

Finally, she got lucky.

"Found it, Chief! Number Eleven Vierstrasse!" she cried out, looking around for Ambrose. He wasn't there. In a mild panic, she ran back down to the bottom of the street where she'd left him, trying to make his Uber app work.

"Ambrose!" she called out, tripping down the cobblestones in fog mixed with snow, "Ambrose, where are you?"

She saw him.

He was way at the bottom of the hill, about to climb into the rear seat of a shiny black Range Rover with blacked-out windows. She waved, and he saw her. "Hullo!" he cried out. "Stay right there, I'll come pick you up!"

He climbed inside and shut the door.

CHAPTER TWENTY-ONE

"There it is!" she said, leaning forward and putting her hand on the Uber driver's shoulder. "Stop, please, this is number eleven on the right."

The Range Rover coasted to a stop outside a dingy row of indistinguishable shops. They all seemed to be falling down, yet they were crowded together cheek by jowl.

"We found it," Sigrid said. "Can you believe it?"

"Hmm," Ambrose said. He had his nose pressed against the foggy rear window, and he was trying to determine which one was the tiny emporium. He could barely make out MILITARY CURIOSITIES on the window in peeling gold leaf. The place looked abandoned. His spirits sank as he reached for the door handle to exit the Range Rover.

"Let's go," his new partner said, opening her door. "Have you got your gun?"

"Gun? I hardly think that will be necessary, dear."

"Yeah, but you've got it, that's the main thing."

Ambrose ducked out of the snow and tried the front door. Locked, of course. He knocked hard, three times, with no response. "I can't see a bloody thing in there. Can you see anything?" he asked Sigrid.

"Junk," she said, shading her eyes with her hands, her nose to the grimy glass. "Wait! Someone's back there! Coming from the rear of the shop. It's an old woman. Here she is."

They stepped back as the old crone pulled the door open a crack.

"What you want?" she said in a low growl, angry and not hiding it well.

She could not have been four feet tall, and she weighed less than ninety pounds. She had a shawl over her head, which partially obscured her sharp-featured face.

Congreve bowed gallantly from the waist and said, "Guns, madame. We are looking for guns." He then pulled out his solid gold pocket watch and dangled it for a moment before looking at it.

She immediately stepped forward and peered up at this giant of a man. "What kind of guns?"

"My wife and I are collectors. We collect historic pistols from the World War II era, madame. Curiosities, one-offs, things of that nature, as a matter of fact. May we step inside?"

She hesitated a moment, nodded, and stepped back, making room for them to enter. Sigrid let the chief inspector go on charming the proprietress while she had a quick look around. A single dim lightbulb dangled by its cord. The light it cast was negligible, but just enough to see her way around the shop.

There were sagging shelves loaded with antique weapons of every description. Swords, battle axes, knives, pistols, and rifles. All stacked on top of each other in a random jumble.

A pile of defunct (one hoped) hand grenades. Artillery shells stacked like dusty soda bottles. She grabbed the first handgun she saw and held it up for the boss's inspection.

"Look, darling, over here!" she said. "I think this is just what we're looking for!"

Congreve excused himself and made his way through the clutter toward her.

"Yes!" he exclaimed. "That's the one, all right!"

Sensing the first sale in years, the owner rushed over and took the pistol from Sigrid's hand a bit too aggressively.

"This one you like?" she said, as if she rather doubted it.

"We do," Congreve said. "What kind of gun is it?"

"Don't know. Not my business."

"Ah. Whose business is it?"

"My son, his business, not mine."

"May I speak with him?"

"He not here today."

"Too bad," Ambrose said, pulling his billfold out and placing a thick wad of Swiss francs wrapped in a rubber band on the glass counter. "I'm very interested in buying this exotic treasure."

"How much you got?"

"Count it. I think that's ten thousand francs, madame."

"Be right back. You wait here."

She glided away on tiny feet into the darkness at the rear.

"Good work, that gun thing," the chief inspector said.

"Thanks. You, too."

"Shhh! How good is your hearing?" he whispered.

"Twenty-twenty."

"Be quiet. Listen. What do you hear, Sigrid?"

"Some kind of whooshing sound."

"Hydraulic door. What else?"

"Some kind of deep humming. I can almost feel it."

"Air-conditioning. There's a sweatshop hidden back there."

"But how do you—"

"Silence, here they come."

"They? How do you know?"

"Shhh."

Two shadows materialized from the gloom.

"Ambrose, I think it's him," she whispered in his ear. "That's the man, I'm sure of it."

Sigrid froze, her fingers digging painfully into Ambrose's forearm. Surely the man would recognize her. It hadn't been that long since he'd last seen her and —

"How may I help you?" the thin, black-haired man said, walking behind the counter and glancing at the money. He had a skimpy black goatee that needed a trim. His mother stood behind him. She was watching their every move, dark eyes moving back and forth.

Congreve smiled and placed the automatic pistol on the counter beside the money. "My wife wants to buy this one."

"She has very good taste," the man said, looking carefully at Sigrid. "How do you come by such knowledge?" he asked her, squinting in the low light.

Congreve slipped seamlessly in front of her before she could reply. "So sorry. My wife is deaf and dumb. I'm Chief Inspector Ambrose Congreve, Scotland Yard. I'm the one with all the money."

"Yes, sir."

"What's your name, son?"

"Ding Wong," he said, casting a side glance at his mother.

"Pleasure, Ding. So. What kind of gun is this? It looks very valuable."

"Excellent eye, Chief Inspector. Extremely valuable, sir. Quite old." Visible money always did the trick.

"Quite rare, is it?" Ambrose said.

"Chinese manufacture, sir, 1920s, maybe 1930s. Very limited production, maybe even handmade, home manufacture. Very popular 1911 to 1949, prewar era. Used by Chinese Communist soldiers. Exposed trigger, so later model. In use because of the arms embargo imposed on us before the war. Five-digit serial number on barrel, but maybe not mass production. Chambered for Mauser 7.63mm."

"Very impressive," Congreve said, hefting the weapon in his hand.

Ding turned his attention back to Sigrid. "This is gun you were looking for, yes?"

Sigrid nodded yes.

"Sold," the tall man said, sweeping the cash from the counter and into his cash drawer. "Thank you. Have to go now."

He turned and nodded to his mother, who took his place at the counter. Then he headed for the rear.

"Hold on a second, Ding," Congreve said. "There's another pistol that I'm very interested in."

"Another pistol, sir?" He stopped and turned around. "Which one?"

"This one."

Congreve already had the Ruger 9mm automatic aimed at Ding's head.

"Huge stopping power, ball rounds," Ambrose said. "Take your arm off. No manual safety, striker fired, short, light, and crisp trigger pull, magazine loaded with seven rounds, hollow points. Care to see how it shoots, Ding?"

"You get out of here. Now. Wife, too. I call police!"

"Good luck with that. Detective Kissl is now going to check you and your mother for weapons. If you even think of resisting, I'll blow your bloody head off. Same goes for Mommy dearest over there in the shadows. Understand me? Because I will do it."

Ding Wong's black eyes flared defiantly, but he nodded his head yes.

"Pat them both down, Detective," Ambrose said to Sigrid.

She moved quickly behind the counter, saying, "Hands in the air. Both of you. Now! Spread your legs. Wide. Did you not hear me? I said *now*! And keep your fucking hands up where I can see them."

Ambrose could not help himself.

He smiled at his new pupil.

CHAPTER TWENTY-TWO

"He's clean, Chief Inspector."

Congreve slid two pairs of plasticuffs toward her and said, "Cuff them both, please, Detective Kissl."

"I found this under the mother's shawl, sir," she said, coming around the counter to hand Ambrose a very lightweight assault rifle, fitted with a silencer.

"Another interesting gun," Ambrose said, smiling at Ding while checking the rifle's magazine. "Take a look. Russianmade SR-3 Vikhr fitted with a SIG Sauer silencer. Extended stock, very light trigger pull. Your mother, too, has excellent taste."

The woman spat twice on the floor.

"How charming your dear mother is. Take good care of this, Detective Sergeant Kissl. It's loaded with twenty highcalibre rounds and set on semiautomatic fire. No safety. Just point and shoot. If you need to, of course."

"Thank you, sir. I've got the mother, you take him."

Sigrid had the assault weapon trained on the old woman now, so Congreve reached across the glass and grabbed the suspect by his skinny neck, yanking him forward so that he was stretched forward across the countertop until his feet left the ground. Ambrose pressed the muzzle of his pistol into the soft tissue between the man's eyes. "What do you know about the death of Leo Hermann?"

"Nothing."

"Try again."

"I knew him, sure, but I didn't actually kill him."

"Well, Ding, I might not actually kill you."

"No dice," Ding said.

"What's going on back there at the rear of the store? The detective sergeant and I want to have a quick look-see."

"Nothing."

"Nothing? You seem like a smart enough fellow. Did you not know that high-ranking British diplomats and Metropolitan Police officers are exempt from prosecution for homicide?"

"Bullshit."

"Listen to me, you little prick. No matter what happens from here out, you and your mother are going to prison for a long, long time. I know exactly who you are and what you have done. Detective Sergeant Kissl can positively identify you. So, here's what I'm offering. Either you take me back there, get me inside your operations room, and give me the information I'm here for . . . or I have the *Stadtspolizei* arrest your mother and remove her to a location where I will make dead certain you'll never see her alive again. How does that sound"

"Bullshit."

"So, make a decision, Mr. Wong. Either say you'll cooperate fully with my investigation from here on in and I'll see what I can do for your lovely mum. Or say good-bye to your mother right this second and tell her you'll see her in the hereafter. Pick one. That's my final offer."

Ding's shoulders slumped and he looked over at the old woman.

"Sorry, Mother."

"You weak! You loser!"

"I will show you."

"We'll be right back, dear," Ambrose said, winking at the mother as he passed her by.

It was a sweatshop like you might find in the financial backwaters down near the docks of old Shanghai. Semi-dark and dreary. Twenty or thirty frantic Chinese moneyboys on their iPhones, moving massive sums of currency and gold certificates around the world and back, packed inside a fifty-by-sixty-foot freezing cold room packed to the gunwales with mainframe computers and workstations, with three or four attractive young women running around delivering coffee and collecting trade chits.

The second the steel door hissed open and Ding entered the room followed by fellow rotund Englishman with a gun in the middle of his back, the room went dead quiet.

"Tell them what you're going to tell them, son. In Mandarin so I can be in on the joke. Do it now."

"Attention everyone," Ding said in Chinese, "The man with me is a British police detective. In exchange for our full cooperation, he is willing to protect us to the extent that he can. That's in case there are any charges against me, or any one of you. Now he is going to ask you some questions. Each of you will answer truthfully, and in clear, loud English. Is that fully understood? Say nothing if you don't understand, stay silent if you do."

The room remained dead silent.

"You're good, son," Ambrose said, slightly amazed at the man's sudden transformation into a serious, well-educated businessman.

"I am a man of my word."

"So am I. First question. Ask them if they, or anyone they know, is aware of foreign nationals hacking into the protected private accounts of British citizens, or primary accounts held in trust for Her Majesty's government or for Her Majesty, Queen Elizabeth, herself. Tell them to raise their hands if they are aware of these recent cyber-attacks on Swiss banking."

Wong translated and said, "Answer by raising your right hand."

Six hands shot up immediately.

Ambrose said, "You six men please rise and go stand along the far wall."

They did so, and Ambrose continued, with Ding's translation.

"Are any of you, or anyone that you may be aware of, working in collusion with foreign agents who may be hacking into protected Swiss bank accounts and property holdings, such as gold, silver, platinum, or other valuable commodities?" Wong translated.

Four hands went up.

"Please join your colleagues at the rear." Wong told them

the next translation. "There is a man residing in Switzerland with whom Scotland Yard detectives would like to have a word. He uses the code name Sorcerer. Are you, or is anyone you know, aware of this man?"

Two hands.

"You two remain standing and stay where you are. Thank you, your help will be recognized by the courts. Final question. Do you two gentlemen who admit to knowing the Sorcerer know the location where he can be found?"

No response. Ambrose looked at Ding. "Tell them again."

"I'm going to repeat the question. Remember that if you do not respond truthfully, evidence will be brought against you that will result in prison sentences of not less than twenty years."

Nothing.

"You've got thirty seconds to stay out of jail. Starting . . . now . . . twenty seconds . . . fifteen . . . ten . . ."

Ding Wong had started shaking, and sweat was pouring down his face. As Ambrose's clock ticked down, Ding's own hand began to slowly rise into the air. "I know who he is."

Ambrose removed his pistol from the small of Ding's back and holstered it. Then he gently asked the suspect to turn around and face him.

"Thank you. You are a much smarter man than I gave you credit for. I will need you to come with me and give your sworn testimony about any information about the man known as Sorcerer. Detective Sergeant Kissl has already contacted local police, and they are on their way. They will take these men into custody. Those who cooperated will all receive due process, just as I said. Do you have anything more to say?"

"And my mother?"

"I'll make sure she's well taken care of, son. One last thing before we go. You say you know the Sorcerer. You say you know his current location. Tell me where he is now and save yourself a whole lot of unpleasantness when we arrive at *Stadtspolizei* headquarters."

Ding confessed all, tears running down his cheeks.

Later, in the interrogation room at police headquarters, Ding Wong and his employees told Ambrose and the police everything they wanted to know.

Case closed.

Almost.

Chapter Twenty-Three

Everything was going according to plan. Alex, a fine natural athlete, was responding brilliantly to the practice climbs and extreme physical training. Luc Bresson had put many climbers through the rigors of a major ascent preparation in short order, and Hawke was performing at an even higher level than Luc had expected, given Hawke's somewhat . . . hedonistic lifestyle. After a week, he told Luc that the air at Base Camp now seemed thick and rich and deliciously saturated with oxygen.

It was a good day on the mountain. Storms were expected later this evening, but for now it was almost pleasant up at Camp Bivouac. Hawke was on his cot, reading a worn paperback called *A Purple Shroud For Dying*. He was recovering that afternoon from intense physical exertion and a recurring battle against altitude sickness.

Luc Bresson stuck his head into Alex's tent at five o'clock that afternoon and said, "Bonjours Monsieur! Ca va?"

Alex raised his head up and said, "Hey, Luc, what time is it? I must have fallen asleep. What's up?"

"Are you available for comms? There's someone on the camp radio who wants to talk to you. Is it okay?"

"Depends on who it is. Is it Sigrid?"

"I am sorry, no."

Alex put his head back down on the pillow and closed his eyes.

"She's the only one I want to talk to. Sorry."

"It's Chief Inspector Congreve calling. He is at the *Stadtspolizei* building. He says it's most urgent."

"Good. Something must be happening down there. Please tell him I'll be there in two minutes."

"Alex?"

"Right here."

"I've got some very good news. We finally caught a break. A banking friend of Sigrid's Jon Levin, with Credit Suisse Security Systems came up with the name of a potential hacking suspect. Former bank employee, forensic accountant who'd left under a cloud."

"Here we go."

"Right. He was running a high-pressure, secret sweatshop in Chinatown. Sigrid and I went there and managed to apprehend him. We got him to agree to cooperate fully in the investigation. As well as his entire staff."

"Wow. Good on you. Sigrid too?"

"You'd have been proud of her. Magnificent job. I'm thinking of taking her on as my personal assistant. At any rate, with the help of the police, we were able to extract the information we've been looking for. The exact location of Sorcerer."

"Amazing. Where the hell is that old devil?"

"Roughly ten thousand feet above your head. Just look straight up"

"Jesus, Ambrose. The Bat Cave?"

"Hmm. There are two entrances to the complex inside the mountain. Built by Swiss engineers in the Nazi era. One of them is below the surface of Lake Zurich. A hundred yards offshore, and about fifty feet below the surface. The other is a secret door, camouflaged by faux granite boulders. It's on the ledge where Lieutenant Christian Hartz landed after his fall. Where he discovered the corpse."

"Just above the Murder Wall?"

"Precisely. You're going to have to climb that bloody wall again, I'm afraid, Alex."

"Luckily for us, I'm not afraid. Luc just told me he thinks I'm all systems go. At first light."

"Very good, Commander Hawke. My assistant and I both wish you Godspeed."

"How is Sigrid doing?"

"You won't recognize her when you get back. She appears to be infused with some new spirit. Quite phenomenal, actually. It seems as if the notion of fear has flown from her vocabulary. Ready to tackle just about anything, actually."

"Is it real?"

"Oh, I daresay it's completely real, Alex. And I'm being very serious about this. A transformation of sorts. I think she hated her job at the bank. Completely unsatisfying for a woman of her intellect and aspirations."

"Where is our heroine just now?"

"She just rang to see if I'd heard from you. She's at home,

preparing to go out. We're meeting for dinner at Cafe Du Jours. Eight o'clock this evening. We shall drink to your very good health. Perhaps I'll even spring for a bottle of Cristal 1953 and Beluga caviar."

"So sorry to miss it."

"We'll do it all over again when you come home."

"I'm going to call her now. Listen, Ambrose, I cannot thank you enough for what you've done. Taking such good care of her, I mean, and cracking the case."

"Thank her. I couldn't have done it without her."

"Gotta run."

"Quickly, Alex, what are they saying about the weather up there tomorrow?"

"Ideal."

"Meaning crap."

"I guess I'll find out. If anything drastic should happen to me up there, I hope you'll—"

"See you soon, Alex. Take good care of yourself."

The day dawned red.

Hawke started up the first face at five.

He planned to attack the face in two stages. The first "pitch," in the lexicon of ascent, would end five hundred feet up at a small hollow in the back of the ice flow. It was situated just beneath a large overhang on the wall he'd nicknamed "the Wowie Zowie" during his last climb. A gentle enough way to start, he told himself. Get loose. Start looking for the "zone," the mental space he needed to occupy when it all got deadly serious.

Hawke was carrying a three-eighths-inch climbing rope, one hundred fifty feet long. In each hand he held an ice ax—a thin, six-inch pick attached to a sixteen-inch fiberglass handle—and strapped to the soles of his climbing boots were his crampons. These were sets of two-inch steel picks, twelve per boot. The front two pointed forward from the toe of each foot.

By planting the picks of his ice axes with a series of carefully directed swings, then balancing on the toe spikes of his crampons after kicking them half an inch into the ice, Hawke could haul himself up the sheer face of Wowie Zowie like some overgrown arachnid. It was a technique he'd used since his very beginnings in the Alps, universally known as front-pointing.

Instinctively prudent, he would safeguard his ascent as much as possible. Every thirty feet he would pause to twist in a threaded eight-inch titanium tube with an eye at one end, then clip an aluminum snap-link called a carabiner through the eye. After that it was just a simple matter of clipping the rope trailing from his waist harness through the carabiner, and up you go!

Five hundred feet off the ground, after many arm-withering hours of battling gravity and the brittle ice of Wowie Zowie, he reached the point where the rock overhung his position like a ragged, rotten awning. He scrunched up under the overhang as close as he could get and fired in another screw. Then he leaned out past the lip of the roof, got his axes planted on the underside, and went for it.

He swung out on his arms, cranked off a pull-up, and started front-pointing upward to the ledge. Once on top, he launched himself into the second stage. He was moving upward at a pretty good clip, and then he wasn't. This higher face, he soon discovered, was an infirm concoction, honeycombed with air pockets. He studied the stuff, which, upon closer inspection, resembled Styrofoam more than ice. Not good.

He took a peek below and saw that climbing back down to the ledge would be well nigh impossible. He took a brief moment to consider his next moves. Weather was threatening. He needed to find a place to hunker down soon. So, hoping the ice would improve as he climbed higher, he pushed onward.

It got worse. As he swung his ice axes over and over with burning arms, trying in vain to chop through the deteriorating ice and find something solid to sink his picks into, he found it harder and harder to keep a grip on his tools.

All of a sudden every anchor point he'd placed sheared out, and he found himself "logging some air time," as climbers called the act of falling. He hurtled upside down until the force of the fall plucked his uppermost screw out of the rotten ice like a toothpick out of a cocktail sausage. He fell past the ledge he'd just left and kept falling.

He felt at that moment that he might actually crater.

It was a verb he never used except when he was on solid ground, in some cheery alpine après-ski environment, sharing a laugh and a drink by the fire with a pretty girl. The phrase *crater* is reserved for those unhappy occasions when a climber suffers the misfortune of falling all the way to the ground.

Luck, as was its habit sometimes, was on his side, because the next screw held and he bounced to a stop on the stretchy nylon rope after falling a mere sixty feet, bruised and frightened but otherwise unharmed. He hung there for a while, spinning lazily in space while he thanked any number of his personal deities, including his lucky stars. When that was accomplished, he started hauling up that bloody rope.

Once atop the ledge, he went about the business of making it cozy. Darkness was falling, and it was futile to try and gain any more ground. If the weather held and he got an even earlier start in the morning, he felt he could reach his destination sometime in the late afternoon. If, of course, he had a bit less excitement than he'd had today.

He first checked all of his gear to make sure he'd not lost something vital to his health in the fall. Then he broke out his rations. He devoured them, heated some water with his stove, and had a lovely cup of tea. He stood up and shoveled snow for a while until he'd cleared enough flat space to pitch his tent. He fully intended to enjoy his evening. It had been a long, eventful day, but he'd had far worse. Far, far worse.

But not to dwell on them was the secret of sanity up here, where confidence and a positive outlook could keep you alive. He would sip his chamomile tea to settle himself, watch the red sky go to black and fill with cold, pinprick stars. And then he would read his book, and then he would sleep.

The average mountain tent has about as much elbow room as your average red phone booth in London, with less floor space than a queen-sized bed. Being tent-bound on a mountain isn't wholly an ordeal. The first hour or two can pass in some dreamy euphoria as you're lying peacefully in your sleeping bag, watching stars come out, or raindrops trickle down from the sky, or snowdrifts slowly climbing the walls around you.

Within the realm of your tiny tent, there is an atmosphere of guiltless relief. The night has blessed you with a sturdy alibi for not risking your life for a few hours. Your life is secure for a while, without anguish or pangs of conscience, or fear.

There is nothing to be done but drift back off to untroubled sleep.

_____

CHAPTER TWENTY-FOUR

He awoke in a state of grace.

He'd opened his eyes to a panoramic view of black eastern skies fading up to faint pink. So beautiful. Even before he rolled over and looked at his watch, he knew he'd changed somehow. While he'd slept, his mind had been hard at work, teaching him, leading him back to truths long lost to him. Yesterday had been far too exciting, simply because he'd been ignoring himself. Not hearing calls from some deeper region of his cortex. Ignoring some old muscle memories anxious to be recalled.

It had almost killed him. If that one last anchor point had failed to hold in the ice, he'd have been sleeping underground. If they'd ever found him. If not, at least he'd have been spending eternity in the company of his grandfather. It was, he thought, actually some consolation.

He knew, before he'd strapped his crampons to his boots, that this day would be different. He felt utterly rejuvenated. In an odd way, he was back. Once properly learned, the sophisticated techniques of climbing, like those of a competitive swimmer, are never really forgotten. All he needed was to re-discover what new limitations aging and inactivity had placed on his skill and nerve. And overcome them.

Contrary to common knowledge, a good climber, with sufficient experience, can move straight up a vertical rock face that he cannot cling to. It's counterintuitive. Human nature dictates a natural desire to cling to anything solid. But a regu-lar, predicted set of moves, from one point of imbalance to its counterpoise, will keep a climber close to the face, but only for so long as he continues moving with speed and grace.

From a distance below, it looks like you're dancing up there. Gracefully careening on and off the wall as you sprint up. It's a skill rather like that of a bicycle rider who has little trouble with balance unless he goes too slowly.

All that's necessary is to first read the pitch accurately, plot out and rehearse the moves cinematically, then make every single move with smooth conviction from hold to hold. Do that, and you will arrive at the next predicted and reliable purchase. And the next.

These skills and abilities had once been Hawke's forte. But during that exciting first day of climbing, he'd made sev-eral misjudgments, one that had caused a serious fall, others that had sent him slithering down twenty feet of scree, bang-ing a little skin off his elbows and doing greater damage to his self-esteem than anything else. It wasn't pretty

The intervening years since his last tragic climb had eroded the fine edge of his physical dexterity. This erosion, he now realized, was beyond repair, even with Luc's valiant ef-forts down at the camp. Today it would be necessary for him to systematically train himself and relearn old tricks while he was up on the Murder Wall. If he wanted to survive, he now had to teach himself to think within the limits of his new, inferior body. He had to learn how to listen to himself.

He set his first pick and hauled himself up.

He was only halfway up the 24,320-foot peak. When he reached the ledge overhanging the Murder Wall, he knew he might find conditions up there worse than at the North Pole. Temperatures could sink to forty below, and winds howled at eighty to a hundred miles an hour. He knew: he'd been given a booklet by the rangers when he'd signed in for his solo climb. Insurance requirement. He'd read that "the combined effect of cold, wind, and altitude may well present one of the most hostile climates on earth." His reaction to those pre-climb caveats was to propose angrily that the rangers mind their own bloody business!

Tomorrow was going to be either a very long day, or a very short one.

But he was no longer afraid of the Murder Wall.

And that was the best guarantor of success that he was going to get when the sun came up.

Seven hours later, he found himself still alive and happy. The Murder Wall had failed to kill him.

The first thing he saw, heaving his body up and over the lip of the ledge, was a small wooden door set in the rock, dusted with fresh snow. Just where it was supposed to be. Until the second he saw it, he was not entirely confident that he'd reached his goal. Visibility was down to almost naught. His altimeter showed he'd reached the designated altitude, but there were other significant ledges of similar sizes above and below him.

This one was called "Das Boot" because it looked like the prow of the massive World War II German battleship *Bismarck*, sticking out the side of the mountain.

The GS on his wrist said that the Bat Cave, if it existed at all, was very near. Reason said this had to be the place. Unless, of course, the Chinese curio shop owner had lied to Ambrose and Sigrid.

The outcropping was wide and deep, and very substantial. Just eyeing it by sight, he'd guess seventy feet across and roughly fifty feet deep. It occurred to him that you could easily get a chopper on and off this thing. He took a few deep breaths to get himself oriented. Out across the far horizon, a sea of ice-topped peaks. The hard part was over. The Bitch had thrown everything she had at him. She'd killed his grandfather and she'd just tried to kill him too.

But this time she'd lost.

The Wicked Bitch was dead. He turned his attention to the escape door. Weathered by the fiercest storms on the planet for a century or more. Wide, and just high enough for him to enter without ducking. At this point, he was simply looking for a way inside the rock. He was searching for the Bat Cave. And he was getting close.

He dusted off the snow that had accumulated on his goggles and scrambled to his feet. He scanned the rocks and boulders to either side of the door, and also above it. He knew what to look for. "Granite2," Blinky had called the material used to hide fighter squadrons and battalions from prying enemy eyes. "You won't know it even when you're staring at it," he'd said. If there was any fake rock on this ledge, Alex sure as hell didn't see it. And even if it was right in front of his face, it was so artfully created that it was virtually indistinguishable from the real thing. He pulled the old iron ring mounted on the door. Wouldn't budge. Too much snow and ice accumulation down at the base. He got his trenching shovel and went to work.

It still wouldn't open, so he got out his chopping ax and knocked out a section wide enough for him to peer inside. When he did, he gagged. Not the smell of death, the smell of old fetid engine oil. What the hell?

He leaned further inside and flipped on his flashlight. No one had been here in fifty years. More likely, never. Maybe never.

It took him a long time to identify the faux part of the mountain. He chopped away with his ice ax everywhere he could reach or see. Nothing doing. His arms burning with the fresh exertion, he dropped his ax to the ground to take a breather and leaned against a heavy boulder. The strangest thing happened.

It moved.

Chapter Twenty-Five

He found himself inside a mammoth cave carved out of rock. There was that same smell of engine oil and machinery he'd experienced inside the empty escape tunnel. He whistled aloud.

It was nearly the size of a United Airlines hangar at JFK. With his first step forward, four beefy characters in black uniforms materialized out of the gloom, all carrying serious assault weapons trained on him. "Morning gents," he said, "Thought I'd drop by and say hello to the Sorcerer. He around? If not, no problem. I could just stop by later."

He heard a deep rumble far back in the cave and looked up. Something was moving forward on the rail tracks in the stone floor.

Seeing a huge black muzzle emerge first, he held his breath. It simply wasn't possible, but there it was. A massive German 88mm cannon. He'd only seen one like it before, and that was in the movie *The Guns of Navarone*. The one the Germans had set inside the tunnel on top of a mountain. Seriously?

A woman made her way down some steel stairs toward him. She had come from a glassed-in office that loomed up over his head. "No need to roll out the heavy artillery," he said. "Hell, I'm not even armed."

"Hello," she said sweetly. "You must be Lord Alexander Hawke, correct?"

"Sorry?" he replied.

"We were expecting you, actually. You're a bit late."

"Hold on. How on earth did you know I was coming, if I may be so bold?"

"Doesn't matter. We heard a rumor. We hear them all the time. I'm the administrative secretary here, Gisela Bundt."

"Rumors about me? From whom?"

"An old friend of ours in Zurich. Look at you, you're shivering. Let's get you some clean dry clothes, a nice cup of tea, and a bite to eat. We're all having goulaschesuppe today. Sound good? Then I'll escort you to the office."

"Whose office?"

"Don't be coy, Lord Hawke. You know very well whose office."

Twenty minutes later, well-fed and wearing dry clothes the woman had provided, he was sitting alone in a large paneled office with Persian rugs and walls studded with Old Masters. Bookcases everywhere, filled with leather-bound collections of authors from Voltaire to Dickens to Hemingway.

Hawke had been told by a green-jacketed servant who'd ushered him inside that someone would be with him shortly. Won't be ten minutes, he'd said. Antsy, Hawke got up from his chair and walked around a bit. Intensely curious, he went over to the source of the light that filled the whole room.

Soaring floor-to-ceiling windows reached to a twenty-foot ceiling, lead-paned and crystal clear.

He was wondering if that massive window was such a good idea, especially for someone trying to remain invisible to the world. That was until he saw the massive steel doors to either side, their exterior surfaces sheathed in hyperrealistic fake rock. Doors that would instantly seal tight at the press of a button. Trying unsuccessfully not to be nosy, he surveyed the rest of the surreally beautiful office.

He checked the fellow's desk first, a large partner's desk in the style of the famous British architect Robert Adam. There were papers casually lying about, but Hawke chose not to look. But brilliant sunlight streaming through the clouds lit up a shiny object that caught his eye. He bent and looked closer. It was a mounted piece of sculpture, about a foot high. He picked it up.

It was a Nazi swastika, carved out of a block of highly polished steel.

He heard a voice behind him and whirled around as if he been caught snooping. "So sorry," he said, putting the artifact back where it belonged, feeling guilty for no reason.

"Not at all," the elderly gentleman said. "Sorry I'm tardy, been a busy day, you know. Please, have a seat."

He strode across the carpet and sat in the leather armchair with its back to the spectacular views. Hawke sized him up very quickly. This was no banker. He was a scholar, perhaps a university professor. He had a natural way and a cheery manner that suggested a facile mind and a quick wit. There was a spark of humor in his blue eyes, fringed with bushy white eyebrows. His head was bald, and he wore a pair of gold eyeglasses that were clearly antique.

He was dressed like a banker, however. A three-piece navy suit from a very good tailor, a crisp white shirt, and a blue-and-white polka-dot bow tie in the manner of Churchill, whom he resembled in an odd way.

He sat back, placed his folded hands on the expanse of green leather, and said, "I must say it's a great pleasure to see you again, Alex. It's been an awfully long time."

Hawke hid his surprise and said, "See me again?"

"Yes. You wouldn't recall, I was just trying to be clever. I led the Swiss Army team that brought you down after that awful fall. And, later, the one that went up for your grandfather. What a lovely man. We've likely never seen his like again."

"Forgive me, this is a bit startling. You two knew each other?"

"We climbed together for years before you were born. Being in a tent with a man on top of a mountain normally brings out the worst in a man. But your dear grandfather and I always had a hell of a time!"

Hawke laughed at that. "I would like to express my gratitude, but I don't know your name, sir."

"Gerhardt, Dr. Gerhardt Steinhauser," he smiled, "sometimes known, rather foolishly, as 'the Sorcerer.'"

"You're not quite what I expected, Dr. Steinhauser."

"Everyone says that, Alex. Few make it to that chair you're using, but everyone who does says exactly that. What do you think of my office? I've grown fond of it."

"It's stunning, sir. I can't help but ask who built all this. A German, I imagine, based on the eighty-eight millimeter that welcomed me."

"Not to mention this paperweight I saw you admiring. The man who built this left behind many mementos when he died.

"And a German indeed. A former Nazi Kriegsmarine admiral who defected to Switzerland before the war. Someone who dabbled in engineering and architecture. I'm sure you've seen Hitler's Eagle's Nest. Same fellow built both. He constructed all this after defecting to Switzerland in 1936. That monstrous eighty-eight you just saw was smuggled onto a train out of Berchtesgaden before people were paying too much attention to the border, you see. His idea was to use it in the event of a German invasion that never happened. Now it's mine, to use as I see fit. Good for nosy neighbors, no?"

"Thank you for all your courtesy, sir, both my rescue and now. I don't want to interrupt what is certainly a very full agenda, but I would appreciate your patience while I ask a few questions?"

"Fire away, my boy, fire away!"

CHAPTER TWENTY-SIX

"Would you mind if I had one of those cigarettes, Dr. Steinhauser?"

"Not at all, help yourself, should have offered. That silver eagle is a lighter, by the way. And please don't call me by that pretentious name. Plain old 'Gert' will do. Your grandfather always called me that."

Hawke smiled and said, "So. Here we are. Thank you for your most gracious hospitality. I'm not sure where to start and . . ."

"Start anywhere you please, Alex. I already know most of it, I'm sure."

"Then you obviously already know who I work for."

"I do. Sir David Trulove, chief of British intelligence. MI6, to be precise. You see, I've long had a keen interest in your exploits ever since we lost Sir Richard Hawke. Have an old leather scrapbook with your name on it, to be honest. Le Rosey, Dartmouth Naval College. Royal Navy combat pilot over Baghdad, Chairman of Hawke Industries, Ltd.,

London's Most Eligible Bachelor, sort of thing. And you have a son. Alexei. Congratulations!"

"That's quite miraculous, but thanks, that will save us a lot of time. So, flash forward. My superior at Six, Sir David, asked me to come here to Zurich to investigate some improprieties involving a recent spate of cyberattacks on Her Royal Majesty's Swiss accounts. My colleague Ambrose Congreve, former chief inspector at Scotland Yard, came as well. Sir David mentioned your name as someone who could be helpful and—"

"And he thinks I'm a scoundrel, doesn't he? A criminal mastermind."

"He never said that. He said you were the éminence grise of Swiss banking, living in seclusion. Power behind the throne. He really didn't offer much more than that. Clearly, his first priority is to protect the Queen and the Royal Family, no matter who or what is involved. Including you, sir."

"Of course, Alex. My role is complex, but it has never been nefarious, I assure you. This infernal moniker that follows me around, Sorcerer, implies some kind of evil wizard. I assure you, I am neither wizard nor evil. Nor saint, for that matter."

"Then may I ask what you are?"

"I'm the peacekeeper. Always have been. The sheriff of Switzerland. There is nothing quite so challenging as keeping a lid on the boiling pot that is Switzerland's role in the world economy. We deal with everyone. Most are honest, but not a few would like to bring this whole elaborate system of doing business, built up over centuries, down. Lately, most of those come from the Arab states. Not all, but a few, would like to see our way of doing business, our way of living, cease to exist. Israel has enormous amounts of its treasury here. And so do the sheiks. Mutually assured financial destruction, so to speak."

"You're the guardian, then? The keeper of the flame."

"You could say that. The Chinese and the Russians are even more difficult these last few years. Amazing cyber-weapons, all aimed at a precious few free countries. Western Europe, Britain, the United States, and their allies."

"Would you say that Russia and China are the source of the recent attacks on Her Majesty, not to mention Britain herself?"

"I certainly would. Containing those two vipers takes up the majority of my allotted time. These events you're seeing involving assets of the Royal Family and Her Majesty's government are the most troubling at this moment."

"Any hope of putting a stop to them?"

"Indeed, a great deal of hope. I am in the process of hiring the very best and the brightest computer scientists from around the world and bringing them here to work for us. Students from China, Russia, and North Korea as well. All very hush-hush, as your grandfather used to say. But yes, these efforts are yielding successes. Because of my affection for the Queen, I have taken personal responsibility for leading a forensic cyberthreat team dedicated solely to Her Majesty's financial protection."

Hawke leaned forward, excited. "Is this something I can bring back to MI6? Your personal involvement with settling the Queen's affairs? For Sir David's ears only?"

Steinhauser thought about it for a long moment.

"Please have Sir David call me about that when you get

back to London, Alex. Tell him that I'll discuss that subject with him. Perhaps I'll invite him here for a few days."

"Thank you. He will be vastly relieved to hear it."

"The Queen, however, is not to hear of this, no matter what. Tell him that. Too many people in Buckingham Palace I'd like not to hear about this."

"Of course. There's another matter I'd like to discuss—the bizarre murder of a Credit Suisse banker just returned from London. We found his corpse just below this location."

"Leo Hermann. I'm glad he was found before he was buried beneath the ice. Leo's death was no murder, Alex. It was suicide. Leo, although thirty years younger than I, was a close friend of mine. But he caused me worry. I had him followed in London. He met with some very unsavory characters at the Connaught Grill—suspects involved with criminal events we've been speaking of. Leo had been selling highly classified information regarding my work for Her Majesty. I'd suspected him for quite some time. The meeting in London was Leo's undoing."

"I'm so sorry about all this. Can you tell me about the circumstances surrounding his death? My friend Chief Inspector Congreve finds himself in a highly unusual situation."

"Which is?"

"Perplexed. For perhaps the first time ever."

"I know your friend Congreve by reputation only. I'll be happy to tell you if it will help you put his mind at ease, Alex. Here's what happened. I called Leo at the Connaught in London that night and told him I needed to see him here in my office immediately. The next day. I'm sure he suspected the worst, but what choice did he have? He arrived late the next morning looking haggard and depressed. Desperate, I would say. He was in tears."

"His life was over," Hawke said.

"I suppose it was. He'd admitted everything to his wife. She was leaving him and taking the two children, moving back to Sweden to be near her family. There was really nothing more to say at that point. I picked up the phone to call my pilot, whose helicopter was in a holding pattern waiting to return for the pickup. Leo got up, said thanks for my kindness, and left. My secretary said he'd gone outside to wait for the helo on the ledge."

"He didn't wait."

"When the pilot arrived, Leo wasn't there."

D**r.** Steinhauser suggested taking Alex on a tour of the vast mountain complex. Honeycombed with brightly lit tunnels and passages leading who knew where, banks of gleaming stainless steel elevators providing service from the secret underwater entrance near the bottom of Lake Zurich. They toured the private residence, three floors with interiors that resembled the Duke of Devonshire's historic country home at Chatsworth. A grand, sweeping staircase joined the floors, which boasted the same panoramic windows as Steinhauser's magnificent office.

There were also separate guest quarters built inside the small peak of a lower mountain. Hawke and his host reached them by a lengthy underground tunnel with a small tram running in both directions on a single track.

"I call this house *'Das Kleineberg,'*" he said.

"'Little Peak,'" Hawke said, smiling.

"Good for you, Alex. Some of the German I taught you stuck."

As they strolled down Little Peak's wide corridors and peeked into various guest rooms, sunrooms, and a paneled reading room, Hawke, who was rarely impressed, found himself full of wonder.

"Small and self-contained, more rustic and, to me, more appealing," Steinhauser said. "Here we are, I wanted you to see this room. Leo Hermann's room. I haven't touched it since his death. I was deeply saddened by the pictures of his wife and children in happier times."

"May I have a look inside?" Alex said.

There were two worn leather armchairs facing the windows, and the two men sat down. Hawke looked around at mementos from a life now lost.

"I can see why it makes you sad," he said.

"When a trusted friend betrays you, it is always deeply disheartening. Especially when their betrayal is a result of matters far beyond their control. Leo was a student of mine when I taught economics at New College, Oxford. Brilliant boy, always was. Hired by both Goldman Sachs and Morgan Stanley in New York, shot to the top of both and moved back to Zurich, happy, for all anyone knew.

"I quickly hired him and put him to work. There were problems as time went by. Sketchy attendance, padded expense accounts, complaints from subordinates, you know how it is. There were rumors that his wife was driving him to make more and more money. The well-known never-enough type of spouse. Leo started drinking heavily, too. Then stealing to try to keep her happy. And, finally, selling information. That's the ending of that sad story."

"I'm so sorry."

"Thank you," Dr. Steinhauser said, rising from his chair. "Alex, it's been marvelous connecting with you after all these years. I dearly hope you'll allow me to continue our new friendship. It's gone eight o'clock. Won't you join my daughter and me for a light supper? I can arrange to have my pilot snatch you from the ledge at nine? Sound good to you?"

"Sounds wonderful, sir. I can't thank you enough for what you did for me and my grandfather. And all you're doing now, not only for me personally, but for my Queen and country as well. I'm sure Sir David will put the full resources of MI6 at your disposal going forward. And if there is ever anything that I personally might do to help your investigation, just let me know."

They took a smooth and silent tram ride back to Dr. Steinhauser's residence.

After a minute, Steinhauser broke the silence.

"There is one thing you might do for me," Dr. Steinhauser said.

"Anything, sir."

"I wasn't going to mention this because I did not know how helpful it might be and . . ."

"Please tell me. I can use all the help I can get at the moment, sir."

"Very well. Recently, since your arrival in Zurich, the hacking attacks on your personal accounts have increased dramatically. It's the Russians on the receiving end, and they are the worst, as you well know. I cannot prove it yet, but someone living here in Zurich seems to be working with Moscow. Hacking into your less-protected assets."

"That's certainly a big step in the right direction. My friend Ambrose will be delighted to know that. Do you know who it is? Just give me a name and MI6 will personally remove this chap from our list of worries. Permanently. Who the hell is it, Dr. Steinhauser?"

"Does the name Baron Wolfgang von Stuka ring a bell, Alex?"

Hawke stiffened at the name, shocked. "You've got to be joking. He's the one helping us solve the case! And by the way, what the hell does he have against me?" Hawke said angrily.

"Rumors are there's a woman involved, Alex."

Der Hohenzollern

"More champagne, darling?"

"Just a splash, Alex. No-no, stop!" Sigrid cried.

Ambrose Congreve sat back and smiled at the two of them. He could not remember seeing his old friend so happy. At least not in a very long time. All three of them had dressed to the nines for their Christmas Eve dinner. Hawke and Ambrose resplendent in black tie, Sigrid radiant in a plunging sequined gown of bright Christmas red.

Tomorrow morning, Ambrose and Alex would board Hawke's Gulfstream for the short flight back to London. But tonight the three friends celebrated where it had all begun.

Der Hohenzollern.

All the festive arrangements had been made in secret; Sigrid collaborated with her old co-conspirator in the planning. The two had reserved the small private dining room on the second floor. The hand-hewn wooden room was a masterpiece of nineteenth-century Austrian carpentry. It had a stone fireplace and lead-paned windows with a view of the bustling town square below and the light snow falling softly on this happy Christmas Eve.

Best of all, a glorious Christmas tree stood in the corner. The top branches of dark green fir brushed the vaulted ceiling; all were decorated with red wooden ornaments, and lighted candles gave the place a golden glow. There were two gifts beneath the tree, one each for Ambrose and Alex.

Laughter was mixed with tying up a few loose ends from the week. Wolfie had been arrested by the *Stadtspolizei*, based on hard evidence supplied by an anonymous source. The case had exploded, reverberating across front pages on both sides of the Atlantic. MI6 and CIA were jointly looking into von Stuka's criminal networks in both Moscow and Beijing, originating in the former and routed through the latter. Hawke and Congreve were assisting with the ongoing investigations.

The source was, of course, Dr. Steinhauser. Hawke had insisted that his friend remain hidden deep inside his Bat Cave, his secret work far too valuable to be revealed to the world at large.

Near the end of the dinner, Ambrose asked about Hawke's decision not to continue on to the summit of Der Nadel, Alex's quest to complete the sad search for his grandfather's bones.

"Two things," he'd replied.

"I know you weren't afraid, darling, so why stop?" Sigrid said.

"On the contrary, I was bloody terrified. I think I was in a state of shock going up that Murder Wall. I have no recollection at all of how I bloody did it. Some mysterious part of me took control of my mind and body and got me to the top. It was only laying there on that snowy ledge that I even realized I was safe."

"Why didn't you continue?" Congreve said, "Why didn't you go on?"

"I'm not like my grandfather, climbing at age seventy. I'm too old even now. You might be glad to know I'll never climb another mountain alone."

"I'll drink to that!" Sigrid laughed, raising her glass in a toast.

They clinked glasses and Hawke continued.

"That brave old man is going nowhere now. And I have a hell of a lot of living to do. I have my son to take care of, after all. And a certain woman of my acquaintance who badly needs all the help she can get."

Sigrid laughed to the point where she almost sprayed them both with champagne. "You said there were two reasons, you sexist pig. What's the other one?"

"Tonight," Alex said. "That was the real reason. I was determined up there that nothing would prevent me from spending Christmas Eve here in this room, with two people I care so deeply about."

"Well said," Ambrose replied with glistening eyes.

Sigrid clinked her glass with her spoon and got to her feet. Hawke thought she had never looked lovelier than she did at that moment, standing in the warm glow of the Christmas tree candles.

"Well, we've been busy down here, too, your lordship. Haven't we, Chief Inspector?"

"Oh, right, I haven't mentioned that yet, have I? Well, Alex, it seems I have a new employee. Someone who has demonstrated great courage and a keen interest in the work of the criminalist."

"Really?" Hawke interrupted, beaming at her.

"Really. Sigrid has resigned her position with Credit Suisse. She is moving from Zurich to London, where she will live in the old gardener's cottage at Brixden House in the Cotswolds. There, she will assist me in every aspect of my work during the daylight hours. At night, she will be enrolled at the University of Glouscestershire, having received early acceptance to study criminal law. It is her intention upon graduation to seek employment at New Scotland Yard."

Hawke reached across the table and took her hand.

"How perfectly wonderful," he said, "How wonderful that is."

"I was hoping you'd say that, Alex. I so hoped you wouldn't feel it was somehow presumptuous of me."

"Are you joking, girl? You'll be right down the road. We can go on picnics by the Thames! You'll meet Alexei, too. I'm sure you two will become fast friends . . . it is the very happiest news, darling. What a truly wonderful Christmas gift. I'm so sorry I don't have anything for you and—"

"There is one thing," Congreve said, smiling at them both. "My new assistant and I have a lot of work to do tomorrow. I was wondering if you might find room to find a seat for her on Hawke Air in the morning?"

"You're moving to London now?"

"Lady Mars says the cottage is all ready. The shippers will arrive with my things on Saturday, so—"

"So, we'll all celebrate Christmas together, Alex."

Hawke laughed and said, "I always got to open one present on Christmas Eve. Is one of those boxes under the tree for me?"

"Open it and find out," Sigrid said.

It was.

A messenger had arrived that day with a framed photograph from Dr. Steinhauser. A grainy black-and-white picture he'd found in one of his scrapbooks.

A photograph of Alex and his grandfather, their arms around each other, smiling happily in the sunlight. It was taken early on the morning as they began their ascent of Der Nadel.

"Merry Christmas, darling!" Sigrid said, and kissed him on the cheek.

Keep reading for an excerpt from
Ted Bell's upcoming novel

Patriot

On sale in hardcover
September 2015

PROLOGUE

May 2012

The sixth-richest man in England ducked his head.

Pure instinct, it was. A tight formation of four Russian MiG-35s suddenly came screaming out of the blinding sun, thundering directly over Lord Alexander Hawke's Royal Navy watch cap. Silver wings flashing, thrusters howling, the fighter jets quickly shed altitude and skimmed over his position, their squat air brakes down for landing.

"What the hell?" Alex Hawke muttered to himself. The British intelligence officer was looking straight up as four fighter jets thundered not a hundred feet over his head! MiG-35s in bloody *Cuba?* He'd have to alert his superiors at MI6 London straightaway.

These MiG fighters were the most radical thing aloft these days; their mere presence here on the island of Cuba confirmed one of Hawke's worst suspicions about his mission: the Russians were no longer fooling around playing, the unconvincing role of "advisors" to the aging Castro brothers. Despite Cuba's impending and highly problematic "detente" with America, the Muscovites had clearly returned to this island paradise to stay. And they meant business.

The plain and simple fact was that his imminent mission, if successful, would soon bring about a head-on political collision between Britain, America, and Russia. The true facts about Cuba's double-dealing would soon flare into stark relief, both in the espionage community and on front pages of newspapers around the world. Welcome to sunny Cuba! Welcome to Planet Tinderbox.

And welcome to realpolitik 2012, Hawke thought to himself.

His four-man stick, or assassination team, and their Cuban guide were crouched in the heavy tangle of verdant jungle encroaching on the airfield. His current position was a scant hundred yards or so from the wide white airstrip. In the recent past, he'd noted on his mental pad, all the cracks in the cheap concrete had been patched, crisscrossed with slapdash splashes of black tar, and the uneven surface mostly cleared of choking weeds and overgrowth.

This very long tactical runway had been chopped into the top of the mountain by the Soviets more than a half century earlier, and it certainly looked its age. One famous legacy the Russians had left behind on the island, seriously crappy concrete.

One after another, the fighter planes scorched the far end of the runway. Puffs of bluish-white smoke spurted from the blistered tyres as, with jets howling, the four aircraft landed in sequence. They then taxied in single file to the far boundary of the field. Maneuvering adroitly, the Russian fighter pilots nested wing to wing in the shadows of a few rusty Quonset hangars overarched with climbing vines. An antiquated control tower, also built by the bloody Sovs during a brief warm spell in the Cold War, provided little in the way of shade.

Commander Hawke motioned to his squad as he rose to his feet, squinting against the high hard dazzle of the sky. "Move out," the Englishman said softly, and he and his men melted back into the protective cover of the dense jungle canopy encroaching on the field. He wanted to get closer to that tower. The MiGs were interesting, but they were not what he'd come all the way from Britain to see.

Ten minutes and a few hundred yards later the commandos had relocated; they were now nearly in spitting distance of yet another Russian airplane, albeit one vastly less sophisticated than the four gleaming MiGs. The first new arrival, having landed a scant few minutes ahead of its fighter escort, was now parked on the tarmac, broiling under the intense Caribbean sun.

The nearby control tower, almost completely enwreathed in cascading flowering vines, loomed above the airplane but provided no shade at all. The fact that all the tower windows were either shattered or completely missing and that there were no controllers present up there seemed to be of little concern to the five Russian pilots recently arrived.

Hawke raised the Zeiss binoculars to his eyes and studied this aviation relic from another century. Unlike the four silver MiG 35s, this was a very old number indeed. It was a dilapidated twin-engine Ilyushin 12 transport, at once a venerable and veritable blast from the past. Hawke caught a sudden glimpse of garish color out of the corner of his eye and quickly shifted his focus left.

A vintage Cadillac limo, painted a ripe old shade of lavender, now rolled to a stop a few feet from the starboard wingtip of the IL 12. A small aluminum ladder was hung down from the opened cabin door aft of the wing. One of the uniformed crew, looking very much like a yachtsman in white trousers and a blue blazer, appeared at the aircraft hatchway.

This chap, clearly DGI, the Cuban secret service unit under the control of the KGB, was shielding his eyes from the fierce sunshine and carrying a serious submachine gun. He climbed down the ladder, circled the faded and rusting limo, and bent to examine the driver's paperwork. Apparently finding everything in order, the armed steward called up to another man still aboard the airplane. A big chap in full jungle camo was now standing in the opening in the fuselage. Hawke smiled. He knew the Russian army officer by the nickname given him by his German father. But he had made his real reputation fighting rebels in Chechnya: a savage butcher.

Der Wolf.

The man climbed down the steps to the tarmac with a good deal of athleticism, Hawke noticed. He held a heavy leather suitcase in his hand, but he handled it as if it were a spy novel he'd been reading on the flight. He was a big, bald man, with masses of bunched muscle around his neck and shoulders. His shirtsleeves were rolled up to the elbows, revealing powerful forearms. The whole gristly package came with a right bullet of a head, too, gleaming with sweat.

Hawke zoomed in on the face, on the hooded dark and bushy-browed eyes of the arriving passenger.

He took a good long look at the fellow and then handed

the glasses to his old friend, an ex–Navy SEAL and former New York Jet, a human mountain from West 129th Street in Harlem known by the name of Stokely Jones Jr. A much-decorated counterterrorist for hire, he was oft described by Alex Hawke as "about the size of your average armoire."

"It's him, Stoke," Hawke said. "Ivanov."

Stokely Jones took a quick peek and confirmed Hawke's opinion. There was no doubt. The man they'd come to Cuba to kill had arrived right on schedule.

That night it turned cold in the mountains. From his vantage point in the jungle peaks of the Sierra Maestra, Commander Hawke could see the misty lights of Cabo Cruz, a small fishing village on the northeastern coast of Cuba, on the coastline far below. To the east, a few more such villages were visible from his vantage point. Dim clusters of light scattered along the black coastline, as if tiny gold coins had been flung out by some giant hand.

These were the only signs of civilization visible in the darkness from the mountainside campsite.

Hawke pulled his collar up as he looked seaward. The wind was up, heralding a cold front moving north. He knew from CIA ops briefings in Miami that a tropical storm was brewing up to the south of Cuba. It was headed this way, a cold wind out of Jamaica, drawn northward by warmer Caribbean waters. Hawke swore softly under his breath. Sometimes inclement weather worked in your favor; and sometimes it decidedly did not.

Among the five men living at the makeshift campsite,

the mood around the deliberately low-burning campfire was one of quiet, confident expectation. The tiny village of Cabo Cruz, just below them, was their target tonight. In that village was the man the commando squad been tracking for the last forty-eight hours, ever since the Ilyushin 12 had touched down at the secret airstrip.

His name was General Sergey Ivanovich Ivanov.

He was a high-ranking Russian officer on a mission from Moscow, a much-feared veteran of the Spetsnaz brigade who'd written their names in blood on the killing fields of Chechnya. Special forces, the crème de la crème of Putin's much vaunted advance combat brigades.

Earlier that afternoon, the general, along with two civilian aides cum bodyguards and his plainclothes entourage of advisors, had checked into a seaside hotel called Illuminata de los Reyes, Light of the Kings. They'd taken the entire top floor of the pale-pink-washed building. The general's quarters were on the third floor, a capacious suite with a balcony overlooking the sea. That night before, Sergey had left the French doors open to the wind and waves; at around midnight, he'd ventured out onto the balcony for a last Montecristo cigar and vintage brandy.

Hawke's four-man stick was a British MI6-initiated counterterrorist team, operating in tandem with the CIA. The Englishman's mission, under the direction of Sir David Trulove, chief of MI6, was straightforward enough: travel to Miami, then Cuba, and gather intelligence about Russian operations on the island. And then take out *der Wolf*.

A forward espionage base in North America was long rumored to be under consideration by Vladimir Putin's top generals as a KGB spy outpost. Human intel reports out of CIA Miami indicated scouting had already begun for a prime location on a small island off the northeastern coast of Cuba.

Hawke's joint force of CIA and MI6 commandos had a clear-cut objective: kill the man sent by Moscow to supervise the design and construction of a major Russian military facility on the Isla de Pinos. In 1953, Fidel had been imprisoned at a notorious facility there, a house of horrors built by Batista. And his brother Raúl had recommended the small island to the Kremlin as the ideal location for a major spy base.

Now, the Castro brothers, despite increasingly friendly diplomatic overtures from Washington, had revealed their true colors: despite any rhyme or reason, the Cuban sympathies still lay with Moscow. Sir David Trulove, Hawke's superior at MI6, had once joked to Hawke that *los hermanos* must have missed the memo: "Communism is dead."

Los hermanos, Spanish for "the brothers," was Sir David's pet sobriquet for that notorious pair of tenacious banana republic dictators.

It had been estimated by British-run undercover operatives in Havana that the general's imminent demise would set back top secret Russian espionage initiatives by at least eighteen months to two years. Time sorely needed by the Western powers to get their act together on the new realities shaping the Latin America geopolitical arena.

The CIA/MI6 hit team consisted of four warriors: Commander Hawke himself, ex–Royal Navy; the former Navy SEAL Stokely Jones Jr.; a young ex-Marine sniper named Captain Alton Irby; and a freelance Aussie SAS demolition expert, Major Sean Fitzgerald.

They had picked up a fifth member, a local guide, shortly after they'd arrived. He was a good-looking young kid named Rico Alonso. He was moody and hot-tempered, but Hawke put up with him. Rico exuded complete confidence, something he'd gained through prior dealings with British and American commandos traveling in harm's way. He'd done it all before, apparently with much success. And he had an encyclopedic knowledge of the jungle regions of the central Cuba's mountains that Hawke was in desperate need of.

The stick had been put ashore on the northeastern coast by an American submarine, *Hammerhead*, out of Guantanamo Bay; the insertion location was a small port city called Mayacamas. That had been two days earlier, the night before they'd scouted the airstrip. Since then they'd been tracking the movements of the target, using Rico to gather intel from the village locals about the Russian general's movements, weapons, and sleep habits.

Tonight, *Hammerhead* had returned to the Mayacamas LZ on the coast. The attack submarine was loitering offshore even now, scheduled for a rendezvous with Hawke at 0400 hours this morning. It was a full moon, and the brightness presented its own set of dangers.

Six hours gave the four-man stick and Rico plenty of time to make their way down to the village, suppress resistance, if any, in and around the hotel, and gain access to the top-floor room where the Russian target was now presumably sleeping. The team would assassinate him and then make their way back along the coast to the exfiltration point as quickly as possible.

It all sounded straightforward enough, and in reality, it

was. But war, as Alex Hawke had learned long ago, had its own reality. If things could go wrong, they would. Even if things could not possibly go wrong, things could always find a way. And, sometimes, incredibly, things would go *right* at the very moment when you'd lost all hope. That was just the way it was in the fog of war.

Behind the keening note of the freshening wind, the sea boomed softly at the bottom of the cliffs. Alex Hawke got to his feet, kicked dirt onto the smoldering embers, and began a final check of his automatic weapon and ammunition. He carried a machine pistol and an FN SCAR assault rifle with a grenade launcher mounted on the lower rail. Grenades hung like grape clusters from his utility belt.

"Let's move out," Hawke said softly, putting a match to the Marlboro jammed in the corner of his mouth.

"Time," Stoke said to the other men. "You heard the man."

Stoke, like the others, was surreptitiously watching their leader, his old friend Alex Hawke. Hawke, especially in his muddy jungle camo, was hardly the picture of a typical British lord in his midthirties. To be sure, there was nothing typical about the man. He was, as one of his former Etonian classmates once put it, "a masterpiece of contradictions." He was a British intelligence officer and former Royal Navy combat pilot about whom it had oft been said: the naturally elegant Lord Hawke is also quite naturally good at war.

Now, on the eve of battle, the man grew ever more calm and at peace with himself. He was unmoving, quietly smoking in the flickering firelight, the smoke a visible curl, rising into the cool night air. Stoke alone knew that behind Hawke's wry smile and placid exterior was, after all, a creature of radiant violence.

This man, whom Stokely had befriended twenty years earlier, was a natural leader; equal parts self-containment, fierce determination, and cocksure animal magnetism. Women and men alike seemed drawn to him like water to the moon.

Even in repose Hawke was noticeable, for he possessed the palpable gravity of a man who had been there and back. A pure and elemental warrior, necessarily violent, riveting, nature itself. Well north of six feet, incredibly fit for someone his age, this was a man who swam six miles in open ocean every day of his life.

He possessed a full head of unruly black hair, had a chiseled profile, and sported a deepwater tan from weeks at sea. And then there were those "arctic blue" eyes. A prominent London gossip columnist once declared in *Tatler* that his eyes looked like "pools of frozen rain." She had thus further embellished his reputation as one of London's most sought-after bachelors. Hawke's two vices, Bermudian rum and American cigarettes, were the only two left to him since he'd given up on women.

"Awright, let's hit the road," Captain Irby, said, kicking enough damp earth onto the fire to extinguish it. And the five heavily armed men began to make their way down the seaward face, hacking their way through rugged terrain covered by dense vegetation. Rico first, then Irby, Fitzgerald, Stoke, and, finally, Hawke, covering the rear.

It was slow going.

The trail was switchbacked, snaking down the mountain,

hairpin turns giving on sheer drops. Almost immediately, Hawke began to second-guess the wisdom of taking Rico's advice. For one thing, the trail was very steep and soon began to grow narrow in places. The commandos were forced to use their machetes simply to keep hacking their way forward. Rico offered constant assurances, saying more than once that it would widen out soon. It didn't. Now, it was barely wide enough for passage.

And then it got worse.

Walls of green now pressed in on them from either side, slowing them down even more. Thick, loopy vines and exposed ficus roots underfoot grabbed at their boots. Hawke, having seen Irby suddenly trip and pitch forward, didn't like it one bit. Not that it mattered much now. Retracing their steps and coming down the open face was not an option at this late stage in the mission.

So there was nothing for it. Hawke grimly kept his mouth shut and told the chattering Rico to do the same . . .

Thirty minutes into the descent, the jungle closed in, then narrowed to a complete standstill. They stumbled into an apparent dead end. A tiny space inside a cathedral of hundred-foot-high palms, the fronds chattering loudly high overhead in the stiff winds, the air in the green hollows cool and damp. Rico was slashing at the solid green walls that remained before them, cursing loudly as he flailed away with his ivory-handled machete.

"Look, Commandante!" the young Cuban kid cried out over his shoulder. "All clear ahead now!"

Hawke looked. Rico had disappeared through the now invisible opening he had slashed between two trees in the wall of palms. The squad pressed forward in an attempt to follow his lead.

"Shut that damn kid up, Stoke," Hawke said, using his assault knife to whack at the dangling morass of thick green vines as he, too, tried to follow Rico's path forward. Captain Irby was now in the lead, and he was pulling back elephant leaves and palm fronds, seeking a way forward.

"I don't like this, boss," Stoke said, watching Irby struggle. "Something is not—"

"*Down!* Everybody get fucking *down!*" Captain Irby croaked, turning to face them, his face stricken. Stoke took one look at the man's clouding eyes and knew they were in deep trouble.

"Hey, Captain, you okay, man?" Stoke said to him, reaching out to help. There was so much blood. The man had something stuck in his . . . oh, Jesus, it looked like Rico's ivory-handled machete. It was buried up to the hilt, near the top of Irby's chest, just above his Nomex body armor. Irby's fixed and glazed eyes stared out at nothing, and he fell facedown at Major Fitzgerald's feet.

"Oh, God, I didn't think he would—" the Aussie said, dropping to his knees to see what he could do for his dead or dying comrade.

And that's when the thick jungle surrounding the natural cathedral erupted in a storm of sizzling lead. Heavy machine-gun fire came from all directions, muzzle flashes visible everywhere they looked, rounds shredding the foliage over their heads and all around the trapped commandos. Masses of shrieking green parrots, macaws, and other tropical birds loudly rose up into the moonlit skies in terror as the incoming fire increased in ferocity.

"Get down now! Take cover!" Hawke shouted. He dove left, but not before he heard the young Aussie scream, "I'm hit! I'm hit!" And then he was silent.

"Damn it to hell!" Hawke cried, getting back on his feet to go to the wounded man's aid.

"Forget him, boss! He's gone," Stoke cried out.

Hawke felt a visceral torque in his gut. In a rage, he opened up with both his assault rifle and his machine pistol, firing both weapons on full auto until he'd exhausted his ammo and reached for more. Stoke had his back, the two of them stood there back-to-back, leaning against each other as they spun in unison, unleashing a 360-degree hail of lead with overlapping fields of fire. The thumping roar of Stoke's heavy M-60 machine gun seemed to be having an impact on the enemy hidden in the jungle.

"Gotta be getting the hell out of here, boss!" Stoke said, grabbing Hawke's shoulder and spinning him around. "Back up the mountain! It's the only way . . ."

"Go, go!" Hawke said. He heaved two frag grenades over his shoulder while turning to follow his friend's upward retreat. He'd taken two steps forward when a high-caliber round slammed him in the lower back, spun him around, and dropped him to his knees.

"Boss!" Stoke cried, seeing Hawke trying vainly to get to his feet and firing his weapon blindly.

"Keep bloody moving, damn it!" Hawke shouted. "I'll take care of these bastards. Leave me be."

"Not today," Stoke said.

Stoke whirled around and bent down, firing his weapon with his left hand and scooping Hawke up with his right. He flung Hawke over his broad shoulders and started running flat out straight up the mountain. The giant with his wounded friend tore through the dense foliage as if it didn't exist.

They got maybe a few hundred yards before all hope of salvation vanished. A broad rope net, weighted with stones, was released by three Cuban soldiers perched on branches high in the canopy. The net fell, entrapping the two enemy combatants, driving them to the ground, and ending for good any hope they still harbored of escape.

When Hawke came to, he was gazing into the sweat-streaked face of the Russian general he'd come to Cuba to kill.

Ivanov was bent over from the waist, smiling into his pris-oner's unseeing eyes. His thick lips were moving, his Adam's apple was bobbing up and down, but he wasn't making any sounds Hawke could understand as he drifted in and out of consciousness. Alex blinked rapidly, trying to focus. He saw Stoke out of the corner of his eye.

His friend was bound by his ankles with rough cordage and suspended upside down from a heavy wooden rafter. He appeared to be naked. And there was a lot of blood pooled on the floor beneath his head for some reason. Had he been shot, too, and hung to bleed out? Hawke's own wound was radiating fire throughout his body. He fought to stay awake . . . heard a familiar laugh and looked across the room.

The kid, Rico, was there, too, sitting at a battered wooden table, smoking a cigarette and swigging from a bottle of rum with some other Cuban guards. He seemed to be talking to Stokely out of the side of his mouth. Every now and then he'd get up, walk over to the suspended black man, scream epithets into his bleeding ears, and then backhand him viciously across the mouth with his pistol. A few white teeth shone in the puddle of blood under Stoke's head.

Stoke, perhaps the toughest man Hawke had ever met, was a stoic of the first order. Hawke had never once heard his friend cry out in pain.

Hawke felt a white-hot flare of anger. Bloody hell. He had to do something! He tried to rise from the chair but felt himself slipping away again. He could not seem to keep his eyes open. How long had he been awake? They never let him sleep. No food. Some poisonous water out of a rusty coffee can now and then. It was cold sleeping on the dirt floor of the dank cement building after the sun dropped . . .

They'd both been stripped naked the first night. Allowed to keep nothing but their heavy combat boots with no laces. The bullet was still in Alex's back, and the wound had turned into one hot mess, all right, but he fought to ignore the searing pain and keep his wits about him. He shook his head and tried to remember where he was despite the spiking fever that made straight thinking so difficult.

It was a compound built in a clearing in the middle of the jungle. Palm tree fronds brushed the ground. High wire fences. Dogs. Every evening the Russians came, including General Ivanov. They drank vodka and played rummy with the Cubans. The general and Rico interrogated the two pris-

oners until they got bored with torture and retreated deeper
and deeper into drink.

The worst brutality the two prisoners had endured was
called the "Wishing Well." Every morning at dawn, two burly
guards would march them naked through the jungle to a spot
away from the compound. There, two fifty-gallon drums had
been stacked one on top of the other and buried in the soil.
Hawke and Jones were made to lie down in the dirt beside
the well. One guy would bind each of their ankles to a stout
bamboo pole while the other one kept his MAC-10 machine
pistol trained on both of them.

Then they'd lift them up off the ground by turns and
dunk them headfirst down into the foul, slop-filled hole.
Sometimes for a few seconds, other times for a couple of minutes. Or longer. Neither man knew how long his head would
be submerged. Each would come up sputtering. The hole was
brimming with a fetid stew of urine and feces.

What the Wishing Well actually was, Hawke and Stokely
soon realized, was the Cuban soldiers' latrine.

"I can't take much more of this, Stoke," Hawke said at
dawn one morning, before the guards came for them. "I'm
deadly serious, man. This will break me. I thought Iraq was
bad. But, this? Hell, I'll just start talking, man."

"We are just not ever going to do that, boss."

"I know."

So that morning was different. The two guards arrived
and marched the naked and manacled prisoners outside the
fenced perimeter and single file into the jungle. The Cubanos

laughing and shouting to each other out of habit. Another hot day, another hilarious game of dunk the prisoners head-first into the latrine.

One guard was in front, Hawke right behind him. Then Stoke, then the other guard at the rear with his gun aimed at the back of Stoke's head. No talking allowed for the two captives. Hawke obeyed that rule until they got within sight of the Wishing Well. That's when he said the one word Stoke was waiting to hear:

"NOW!"

In that instant, Hawke got his manacled wrists over the guard's head and cinched tight around the stocky Cuban's throat. Hawke yanked him backward off his feet, got him on the ground, and began pummeling his face with his two bound fists, using the steel manacles as a weapon. Stoke, meanwhile, planted one foot and whirled, whipping his bound hands in a great sweeping arc, slamming his enjoined fists against the side of the other guard's head and knocking him off his feet.

Hawke had little memory of the ensuing skirmish. Both Cubans acquitted themselves rather nicely, knowing full well they were fighting for their lives. Hawke was fairly sure he'd bit both ears off his guy and done terrible things to his eyes and teeth. And, ultimately, to the vertebrae in his cervical spine. C3, C4, and C5, damaged beyond repair.

Meanwhile, Stoke used his enormous size and weight to his advantage. He sat atop the guy long enough to break the index finger of the thrashing right hand by removing his gun while his finger was still inside the trigger guard. Then he bounced up and down on his chest a couple of times until all his ribs fractured pretty much at once. Until something sharp and splintery pierced his heart and lungs.

For three days they fought to survive in the wild. Naked, hungry, no food, no water, no map. They followed the sun during the day. Kept well clear of the occasional dirt roads. Survived on snakes, bugs, and bark. Made a little shelter with palm fronds every night to keep the cold rain off their hides. And so it went.

On the fourth night, they heard booming surf in the distance. That's when they came upon a high wire fence. They had little strength left to go around it. Hawke was in far worse shape than Stokely; he'd lost a lot of blood and still battled a raging fever. Somehow, they both found enough strength to scale the fence and drop to the ground on the other side.

Hawke woke up in sick bay the next morning with no memory of how he'd come to be there.

"Good morning, handsome," a pretty red-haired American nurse said to him, holding the straw in his orange juice next to his parched lips. "There's someone here to see you."

Hawke smiled.

"Who is it?"

"I'll go get him, honey," the nurse said.

Now a strange man appeared at his bedside. American military. Brass, obviously. A U.S. naval officer, who was also smiling down at him in a friendly way. Where the bloody hell was he? On a U.S. destroyer?

"Good morning, Admiral," Hawke managed, very happy to see a familiar uniform and a friendly face.

"Good morning," the old man said, pulling a chair up to his bedside. "Son, I don't know who the hell you are or where the hell you came from, but I will tell you one goddamn thing. You ruined my golf game, sailor."

"Sorry, sir?"

"You heard me. I came up the seventh fairway this morning half expecting to find my ball in a sand trap. Instead, I found you. Bare assed, except for your goddamn shoes. Damnedest thing I ever saw. And no tracks in the sand anywhere around you. Like you'd dropped out of the blue."

"From the top of the fence, Admiral."

"But how the hell did you—Never mind."

"I'm sorry, sir."

"Oh, hell, don't apologize. I hit my sand wedge out of there and sank it for a birdie! Almost had to take your foot off to get my club face on the ball. Never had a human hazard before! Welcome to the Guantanamo Bay Naval Base Golf and Country Club, son! We're glad to have you and your Navy SEAL friend Mr. Jones here as our guests."

Then the admiral laughed and handed him a fat Montecristo cigar. He helped Hawke get it lit and then said, "Tell me, what can I do for you, son? You look to me like a man who could use a helping hand right about now."

Hawke smiled and said, "There is one thing you could do for me, sir."

"Name it."

"Got any drones?" Hawke said, taking another puff and feeling instantly much improved. The fog seemed to be lifting. He saw a small green bird alight on his sunny windowsill, and it seemed to him a harbinger of happy days to come.

"Hell, yeah, I got drones, son. Shitload of them. What exactly do you have in mind?"

"Well, Admiral, you see, there's this little pink hotel over on the northeast coast of Cuba. Place called the Illuminata de los Reyes. One of the guests there, a Russian chap of my acquaintance, was exceptionally rude to my friend Stokely Jones and me recently. Killed a couple of my chaps in an ambush. And I thought, well, perhaps you could teach him a lesson in old-fashioned Anglo-American manners."

"Done and done!" The admiral laughed. "I'll have my guys get a couple of birds in the air before lunchtime. That little hotel you mentioned, that's the pretty pink one over in Cabo Cruz, am I right?"

"That's the one all right, Admiral."

"I'm on it."

And damn if it wasn't done that very day.

Done, and done, as they say.

CHAPTER ONE

You see, the whole damn business started with the USS *Cole*.

The *Cole* is a serious U.S. Navy warship, mind you. Think billion-dollar baby. She's a 505-foot-long Arleigh Burke–class guided-missile destroyer. She carries a vast array of advanced radar equipment, not to mention her torpedoes, machine guns, Tomahawk missiles, and, well—you get the picture. Bad mammajamma.

Big, badass damn boat. Kept afloat by a crew of young navy seamen. And you won't find as nice a gang of fine young men and women as you will in the U.S. Navy. "Yes, sir," "No, ma'am," kids, all of them. Manners, remember those? Good haircuts? Pants actually held up with belts? Yeah, I didn't think so.

Along about August 2000—remember, this was about a year before the attack on the Twin Towers—USS *Cole* sailed from NAS Norfolk to join the U.S. Fifth Fleet in the Arabian Gulf. A few months later she called at the seaport of Aden, situated by the eastern approach to the Red Sea. A city, weird as it might seem, built in the crater of a dormant volcano.

What were they thinking? Anyway, the day it all went down, the Big Wake-Up Call, I like to call it, the *Cole* was under a security posture known as Threatcon Bravo. We're talking the third of five alert levels used by the U.S. Navy to label impending terrorist threats.

Sunny day. Hot as Hades. Most of the crew was busy with daily shipboard routine, but a bunch of guys had their shirts off, sunning on the foredeck, playing cards, shooting the breeze, or, more accurately, the shit, as they say in the navy.

One of the guys, out of the corner of his eye, notices a small fiberglass fishing boat making its way through the busy harbor. Kinda boat local fishermen used to ply their trade around the harbor. Nothing fancy and certainly nothing scary.

The boat seemed to be headed right for the ship's port side, or, so thought Seaman Foster Riggs anyway. Now, on a normal day, you understand, most of the harbor's waterborne inhabitants sensibly gave the *Cole* a wide berth. Which is why Seaman Riggs got up and went to the port rail to have a closer look at the approaching vessel. Something odd about it, he was thinking.

It was going pretty fast for conditions, number one. Two locals stood side by side at the helm station. Young guys, bearded, T-shirts and faded shorts. Had the throttle cranked, the boat up on plane. Out for a cruise, a couple of amigos just having a good time, was what it looked like.

Nothing looked all that out of the ordinary to Riggs, even as the fishing boat drew ever nearer to the *Cole*. Big smiles on the local yokels' faces as they pulled along the destroyer's port side.

As the boat settled, they were raising their hands up in the air, waving hello at the friendly young sailor staring down at them. Friendlies themselves, Riggs was thinking. But then they did something funny, something that should have sounded crazy loud alarm bells banging big-time inside that young seaman's head.

The two men looked up at the skinny sailor on the foredeck, snapped to attention, and then saluted smartly. Riggs noticed something really strange then: the smiles were gone from their faces.

A second later, those two boys were vaporized. They had just exploded a whole boatload of C-4 plastic explosive. At the moment of the explosion, the little skiff was about five feet from the warship's hull. And that much C-4 at close range? Hell, that is the equivalent of seven hundred pounds of TNT blowing up in your face.

The blast shattered windows and shook the buildings along the waterfront. It also opened a forty-foot-by-forty-foot gash in the destroyer's reinforced steel hull. And turned the inside of that ship into an abattoir. Seventeen of our young warriors were killed instantly or mortally wounded. Thirty-nine more were seriously injured. It was bad. It was real bad, brother.

The *Cole* incident, that was the single worst attack on an American target since the 1998 bombings of U.S. embassies in Kenya, Nairobi, and Dar es Salaam, Tanzania.

That attack was bad enough.

And then it got worse.

The blast in the Gulf of Aden sent shock-wave repercussions rolling down the corridors of the Pentagon.

The navy brass had finally gotten the wake-up call heard round the world. Decades of the USN's woefully outdated policies and training procedures had finally come back to bite the navy's ass, big-time. The much disputed Rules of Engagement, well, that's exactly what had put the *Cole* in the cross-hairs of two young terrorists hell-bent on killing American sailors.

And the *Cole*? Hell, she had been a sitting duck. Never had a chance.

Crew members started reporting that the sentries' Rules of Engagement, set up by the ship's captain according to navy guidelines, "would have prevented them from defending the ship even if they'd detected a threat." The crew would not have been permitted to fire *without being fired upon first*! You're beginning to see the problem. But, wait, there's more.

A petty officer manning a .50 cal. at the stern of the *Cole* moments after the explosion that fateful day saw a second boat approaching and was ordered to turn his weapon away unless and until he was actively shot at. "We're trained to hesitate," the young sailor told the board of inquiry. "If somebody had seen something that looked or even smelled wrong and fired his weapon, sir? That man would have been court-martialed."

The commander of the U.S. Navy's Fifth Fleet concluded: "Even had the *Cole* implemented Threatcon Bravo measures flawlessly, there is total unity among the flag officers that the ship would not and could not have prevented or even deterred this attack."

Hello?

Now you got yourself a Class A shitstorm brewing in the Pentagon. Now you got the commander of the Fifth Fleet—

which patrols five million square miles, mind you, including the Red Sea, the Arabian Gulf, the Arabian Sea, and parts of the Indian Ocean—saying, hold on, a U.S. Navy destroyer versus a crappy little fishing boat? And the fishing boat *wins*?

That's when the call for help went out. And that's where I come in.

My outfit, a little ole Texas company at that time, called Vulcan Inc., was just one of many providers contacted by the U.S. Navy and the Department of Defense. They wanted to see just how quickly people like me could respond to their "urgent and compelling" need for the immediate training of twenty thousand sailors in force protection over the next six months. The navy was basically saying to all of us, *Look, we have to train X number of sailors at X types of ranges and we need to do it now. Can you handle that?*

My name is Colonel Brett "Beau" Beauregard. I'm the founder and CEO of Vulcan Inc. And I knew this was my shot. Mine was the only company that checked every box on the navy's list. At the time, I had only twenty full-time employees. At Vulcan's original training facility on the Gulf of Mexico south of Port Arthur, Texas, hell, we hadn't even trained a measly three thousand people.

That was the total ever since opening our doors three years earlier. But Beau? Nothing if not aggressive. First in my class at West Point, decorated U.S. Army Ranger, strong as a team of oxen, captain of the Army gridiron team that beat Navy to win the Thanksgiving Army-Navy game my senior year.

Go, Army! And as I always say, "It ain't braggin' if it's true."

That navy contract? It was worth over seven million dollars. I was worth about seven cents. And I had only thirty days to get my guys ready. I got myself started bright and early next morning, you better believe I did.

I began construction on a little idea I'd cooked up called a "ship-in-a-box." It was a floating superstructure made of forty-foot steel tractor-trailer containers. It was painted battleship grey and fitted with watertight doors and railings. Imagine an elaborate ship's bridge on a movie set, but one designed to withstand live ammunition in real-life firefights. Stone cool.

For one month, no one around here slept much. But the old colonel's magical training boat-in-a-box was ready for the navy when day 30 rolled around. To my great surprise, and delight, Vulcan won that damn navy contract. Over the next six months down at Port Arthur, Vulcan personnel trained nearly a thousand new sailors a week! We taught them to identify threats, engage enemies, and defeat terrorist attacks while aboard ships either in port or at sea.

Almost immediately, I identified one of the navy's biggest problems. This was the original gang that couldn't shoot straight! It had been maybe years since a whole lot of these guys had even held guns in their hands. U.S. Navy sailors who had never even used a firearm since boot camp!

Hundreds of sailors started flowing through the facility every week. The ATFP approach developed by my team, Anti-Terrorism Force Protection, was the very finest available on the planet at that time. We ramped up the manning, training, and equipping of naval forces to better realize a war fighter's physical security at sea. ATFP became the U.S. Navy's primary focus of every mission, activity, and event. This mind-set was instilled in every one of the sailors who went through the program.

Vulcan was so successful that in 2003, Vulcan would train roughly seventy thousand sailors at our rapidly growing Port Arthur, Texas, facility.

One night I told my brand-new wife, Margaret Anne, I felt like that scrappy little dog who finally caught that school bus he'd been chasing. We expanded the Port Arthur operation again and again—up to over seven thousand acres, more than twelve square miles, including considerable conservation areas to preserve wetlands and restore wildlife habitat. I made sure we reseeded hundreds of acres with native oak and swamp cypress.

And I made one other important addition to the facility.

I'd shot me a massive black bear over in Red River County east of Dallas. Took that bad boy with a black powder rifle. Old Blackie now stood on his hind legs in the lobby of the main Lodge, a 598-pound symbol of Vulcan's trademark tenacity—jaws frozen open, right paw raised high, ready to strike. It became the corporate logo, on every piece of paper my company generated in the years that followed. I've still got the T-shirt.

In a few short years, Vulcan achieved worldwide fame. We were providing private military assistance to any country that could afford our services. And here's the thing: we did not play favorites, and politics never entered into the equation. I was a soldier of fortune, after all, and this soldier was looking to make his fortune. I was soon working with the military and military intelligence agencies of countries around the world. And not once did I show a trace of favoritism toward any client or any government; that's what kept me in the game.

I got pretty good at building impenetrable firewalls between our clients. The degree of security afforded each major account was so highly regarded that the Americans, the Russians, and even the Chinese were all equally comfortable that their most closely held secrets were safe with us. Hell, at one point early on, Vulcan could claim both Israel and the Iranians as clients at one and the same time!

My own journey to the pinnacle of power had begun; and neither America nor, later, the world, had a clue what they were in for. I made it to the very top, and I clung to my position tenaciously. But the center would not hold. Events, politics, politicians, and most devastating of all, the media, overtook me in the end. The whole world would turn on me, viciously, and bring me down.

Because in the end, me and my guys, the former heroes of Vulcan, we who had taken bullets for the Americans and everyone else, would become objects of scorn and ridicule in the press and everywhere else. And many believed it was all through no fault of our own. Hell, I believe it to this day! Did some innocent people get shot? Yeah, it's called war. Did we shoot first? My opinion? No, we did not. I've seen the evidence. I stand by my troops to this day.

First America, and then the rest of the world, like dominoes, threw Colonel Beauregard under the bus. My men were labeled wanton murderers in the world press. Cowboys with neither scruples nor morality. Hired killers who would turn on anyone if the price was high enough. Eventually, the old colonel disappeared from the front pages of the media . . . some said I was only biding my time. Some said I wanted nothing to do with the world anymore and had gone into seclusion in some remote location down in the Caribbean. And that's just what I damn well did.

Now, here comes the funny part.

That I would return to the front lines one day in the not too distant future, exponentially more powerful than ever before, was unthinkable at that dark time. Or that I would seek my ultimate revenge on a duplicitous world that had shamed me, nearly destroying me.

As it all turned out in the end, Vulcan's rapid fall from grace and glory was not the end of me. Not by a long shot. As one of my hardasses said when he saw me back in a Jeep, "The colonel has definitely not left the building."

In fact, all this ancient history I been telling you? It was only the beginning of my story.

Respectfully Submitted, November 2015
Colonel Brett T. Beauregard, U.S. Army, Ret.
Aboard *Celestial*
Royal Bermuda Yacht Club
Hamilton, Bermuda

CHAPTER TWO

Paris
April 2015

Most evenings, like tonight, Harding Torrance walked home from the office. His cardiac guy had told him walking was the best thing for his ticker. Harding liked walking. He even wore one of those FitBit thingamajigs on his wrist to keep track of his steps. Doctor's orders after a couple of issues popped up in his last stress test. But the truth was, Harding liked walking in Paris, especially in the rain.

Ah, April in Paris.

And the women on the streets, too, you know? God in heaven. Paris has the world's most beautiful women, full stop, hands down. The clothes, the jewelry, the hair, the way they walked, the posture, the way . . . the way they dangled their dainty little *parapluies*, the way they goddamn *smelled*. And, it wasn't perfume, it was natural.

Plus, his eight-room Beaux-Arts apartment was an easy stroll home from his office. His ultradeluxe building was located on the rue du Faubourg Saint-Honoré, right next to Sotheby's. Saint-Honoré was the shopping street in one of the fancier arrondissements on the Right Bank. Where there are beautiful shops, there are beautiful women, *n'est-ce pas?* Especially in this extremely ritzy neighborhood. Or arrondissement, as the froggies like to say.

Tell the truth, he'd lived here in Paris for ten years or more and he still didn't have any idea which arrondissement was which. Somebody would ask him, *Which is which?* He'd shrug his shoulders with a smile. He had learned a handy little expression in French early on which had always served him well in his expatriate life: *"Je ne sais pas."*

I don't know!

At any rate, his homeward route from the office took him past the newly renovated Ritz Hotel, Hermès (or "Hermeez" as the bumpkins called his ties whenever he wore one when he visited Langley), plus, YSL, Cartier, et cetera, et cetera. You get the picture. Ritzy real estate, like he said. And, just so you know, Hermès is pronounced "Air-mez."

Very ritzy.

Oddly enough, the ritziest hotel on the whole rue was not the one *called* the Ritz. It was the less obvious one called Hôtel Le Bristol. Now, what he liked about the Bristol, mainly, was the bar. At the end of the day, good or bad, he liked a quiet cocktail or three in a quiet bar before he went home to his wife. That's all there was to it, been doing it all his life. His personal happy hour.

The Bristol's lobby bar was dimly lit, church quiet, and hidden away off the beaten path. It was basically a dark paneled room lit by a roaring fire situated off the lobby where only the cognoscenti, as they say, held sway. Harding held sway there because he was a big, good-looking guy, always impeccably dressed in Savile Row threads and Charvet shirts of pale pink or blue. He was a big tipper, a friendly guy, great smile. Knew the bar staff's names by heart and discreetly handed out envelopes every Christmas.

Sartorial appearances to the contrary, Harding Torrance was one hundred percent red-blooded American. He even worked for the government, had done, mostly all his life. And he'd done very, very well, thank you. He'd come up the hard way, but he'd come up, all right. His job, though he'd damn well have to kill you if he told you, was station chief, CIA, Paris. In other words, Harding was a very big damn deal in anybody's language.

El Queso Grande, as they used to say at Langley.

He'd been in Paris since right after 9/11. His buddy from Houston, the new president, had posted him here because the huge Muslim population in Paris presented a lot of high-value intel opportunities. His mandate was to identify the al-Qaeda leadership in France, then whisk them away to somewhere nice and quiet for a little enhanced interrogation.

He was good at it, he stuck with it, got results, and got promoted, boom, boom, boom. The president had even singled him out for recognition in an Oval Office reception, had specifically said that he and his team had been responsible for saving countless lives on the European continent and in the United Kingdom. What goes around, right? Let's just say he was well compensated.

Harding had gone into the family oil business after West Point and a stint with the Rangers out of Fort Bragg. Spec-ops duty, two combat tours in Iraq. Next, working for Torrance Oil, he was all over Saudi and Yemen and Oman, running his daddy's fields in the Middle East. He was no silver spooner, though; no, he had started on the rigs right at the bottom, working as a ginzel (lower than the lowest worm), working his way up to a floorhand on the kelly driver, and then a bona fide rig driller in one year.

That period of his life was his introduction to the real world of Islam.

Long story short?

Harding knew the Muslims' mind-set, their language, their body language, their brains, even, knew the whole culture, the mullahs, the warlords, where all the bodies were buried, the whole enchilada. And so, when his pal W needed someone uniquely qualified to transform the CIA's Paris station into a first-rate intelligence clearinghouse for all Europe? Well. Who was he to say? Let history tell the tale.

His competition? Most guys inside the Agency, working in Europe at that time, right after the Twin Towers? Didn't know a burqa from a kumquat and that's no lie—

"Monsieur Torrance? Monsieur Torrance?"

"*Oui?*"

"*Votre whiskey, monsieur.*"

"Oh, hey, Maurice. Sorry, what'd you say? Scotch rocks?" he said to the head bartender, distracted, not even remembering ordering this fresh one. "Sure. One more. Why not?"

"*Mais oui, m'sieur. There it is. C'est ça!*"

Apparently his drink had arrived and he hadn't even noticed. That was *not* a first, by the way.

"Oh, yeah. Merci."

"*Mais certainement, Monsieur Torrance. Et voilà.*"

His drink had come like magic. Had he already ordered

that? He knocked it back, ordered another, and relaxed, making small talk, *le bavardage,* with Maurice about the rain, the train bombing in Marseilles. Which horse might win four million euros in the Prix de l'Arc de Triomphe at Longchamp tomorrow. The favorite was an American thoroughbred named Buckpasser. He was a big pony, heralded in the tabloids as the next Secretariat, Maurice told him.

"Really? Listen. There will never, *ever,* be another 'Big Red,' Maurice. Trust me on that one."

"But of course, sir. Who could argue?"

Harding swiveled on his barstool, sipping his third or fourth scotch, depending, checking the scenery, admiring his fellow man . . .

And woman . . .

And this one rolled in like thunder.

CHAPTER THREE

He'd always said he'd been born lucky. And just look at him. Sitting in a cozy bar on a cold and rainy Friday night. He'd told his wife, Julia, not to expect him for dinner. Just in case, you know, that *something came up*. He'd explained to her that, well, honey, something troubling *had* come up. That whole thing with the state visit of the new Chinese president to the Élysée Palace on Sunday? About to go *au toilette!*

"Sorry, is this seat taken?" the scented woman said.

What the hell? He'd seen her take an empty stool at the far end of the bar. Must have changed her mind after catching a glimpse of the chick magnet at the other end . . .

"Not at all, not at all," he told her. "Here, let me remove my raincoat from the barstool. How rude of me."

"Thank you."

Tres chic, he registered. *Very elegant.* Blond. Big American girl. Swimmer, maybe, judging by the shoulders. California. Stanford. Maybe UCLA. One of the two. Pink Chanel, head to toe. Big green Hermès Kelly bag, all scruffed up, so loaded. Big rock on her finger, so married. A small wet puffball of a dog and a dripping umbrella, so ducked in out of the rain. Ordered a martini, so a veteran. Beautiful eyes and fabulous cleavage, so a possibility . . .

He bought her another drink. Champagne, this time. Domaines Ott Rosé. So she had taste.

"What brings you to Paris, Mrs. . . ."

"I'm Crystal. Crystal Methune. And you are?"

"Harding," he said, in his deepest voice.

"Harding. Now that's a good strong name, isn't it? So. Why *are* we here in Paris? Let me see. Oh, yes. Horses. My husband has horses. We're here for the races at Longchamp."

"And that four million euros' purse at Longchamp, I'll bet. Maurice here and I were just talking about that. Some payday, huh? Your horse have a shot? Which horse is it?"

"Buckpasser."

"Buckpasser? That's your horse? That's some horse, honey."

"I suppose. I don't like horses. I like to shop."

"Attagirl. Sound like my ex. So where are you from, Crystal?"

"We're from Kentucky. Louisville. You know it?"

"Not really. So where are you staying?"

"Right upstairs, honey. My hubby took the penthouse for the duration."

"Ah, got it. He's meeting you here, is he?"

"Hardly. Having dinner with Felix, his horse trainer, somewhere in the Bois de Boulogne, out near the track is more like it. The two of them are all juned up about Buckpasser running on a muddy track tomorrow. You ask a lot of questions, don't you, Harding?"

"It's my business."

"Really? What do you do?"

"I'm a writer for a quiz show."

She smiled. "That's funny."

"Old joke."

"You're smart, aren't you, Harding? I like smart men. Are you married?"

"No. Well, yes."

"See? You are funny. May I have another pink champagne?"

Harding twirled his right index finger, signaling the barman for another round. He briefly tried to remember how many scotches he'd had and gave up.

"Cute dog," he said, bending down to pet the pooch, hating how utterly pathetic he sounded. But, hell, he was hooked. Hooked, gaffed, and in the boat. He'd already crawl through a mile of broken glass just to drink her bathwater.

"Thanks," she said, lighting a gold-tipped cigarette with a gold Dupont lighter. She took a deep drag and let it out, coughing a bit.

"So you enjoy smoking?" Harding said.

"No, I just like coughing."

"Good one. What's the little guy's name?"

"It's a her. Rikki Nelson."

"Oh. You mean like . . ."

"Right. In the Ozzie and Harriet reruns. Only this little bitch on wheels likes her name spelled with two 'k's. Like Rikki Martinez. You know? Don't you, precious? Yes, you do!"

"Who?"

"The singer?"

"Oh, sure. Who?"

"Never mind, honey. Ain't no thing."

"Right. So, shopping. What else do you like, Crystal?"

"Golf. I'm a scratch golfer. Oh, and jewelry. I really like jewelry."

"Golfer, huh? You heard the joke about Arnold Palmer's ex-wife?"

"No, but I'm going to, I guess."

"So this guy marries Arnold Palmer's ex. After they make love for the *third* time on their wedding night, the new groom picks up the phone. 'Who are you calling?' Arnie's ex asks. Room service, he says, I'm starved. That's not what Arnold would've done, she says. So the guy says, okay, what would Arnold have done? Arnold would have done it again, that's what. So they did it again. Then the guy picks up the phone again and she says, 'You calling room service again?' And he says, 'No, baby, I'm calling Arnold. Find out what par is on this damn hole.'"

He waited.

"I don't get it."

"Well, see, he's calling Arnold because he—"

"Shhh," she said, putting her index finger to her lips.

She covered his large hand with her small one and stroked the inside of his palm with her index finger.

She put her face close to his and whispered, "Frankly? Let's just cut the shit. I like sex, Harding."

"That's funny, I do, too," he said.

"I bet you do, baby. I warn you, though. I'm a big girl, Harding. I am a big girl with big appetites. I wonder. Did you read *Fifty Shades of Grey?*"

"Must have missed that one, sorry. You ever read Mark Twain?"

"No. Who wrote it?"

"What?"

"I said, who wrote it? The Mark Twain thing."

"Doesn't matter, tell me about *Fifty Shades of Grey*."

"Doesn't matter. I found it terribly vanilla," she said.

"Hmm."

"Yeah, right. That's what men always say when they don't know what the hell a girl is talking about."

"Vanilla. Not kinky enough."

"Not bad, Harding. Know what they used to say about me at my sorority house at UCLA? The Kappa Delts?"

"I do not."

"That Crystal. She's got big hair and big knockers and she likes big sex."

He turned to face her and took both her perfect hands in his.

"I'm sorry. Would you ever in your wildest dreams consider leaving your rich husband and marrying a poor, homeless boy like me?"

"No."

"Had to ask."

"I do like to screw. You do get that part, right?"

"Duly noted."

"Long as we're square on this, Harding."

"We're square."

"I'm gonna tie you to the bed and make you squeal like Porky Pig, son. Or, vice versa. You with me on this?"

He just looked at her and smiled.

Jackpot.

The elevator to the penthouse suite opened inside the apartment foyer. It was exquisite, just as Harding would have imagined the best rooms in the best hotel in Paris might be, full of soft evening light, with huge arrangements of fresh flowers everywhere, and through the opened doors, a large terrace overlooking the lights of Paris and the misty gardens directly below.

Crystal smiled demurely and led him into the darkened living room. She showed him the bar and told him to help himself. She'd be right back. Slipping into something a little more comfortable, he imagined, smiling to himself as he poured two fingers of Johnnie Walker Blue and strolled over to a large and very inviting sofa by the fireplace.

He kicked his shoes off, stretched out, and took a sip of whisky. He was just getting relaxed when he heard an odd streaming sound. Looking down at the floor, he saw that the little fuckhead Rikki Nelson had just peed all over his Guccis.

"Shit!" he said, under his breath.

"Hey!" he heard Crystal yell.

"What?"

"Turn on some music, Harding; Momma wants to dance, baby!" she called out from somewhere down a long dark hall.

He got to his feet and staggered a few feet in the gloom, cracking his shin on an invisible coffee table.

"What? Music? Where is it?"

"Right below the bar glasses. Just push 'on.' It's all loaded up and ready to rip."

He limped over to the bar and hit the button.

Dean Martin's "That's Amore" filled the room.

"Is that it?" he shouted over Dino.

"Hell, yeah, son. Crank it!"

He somehow found the volume control, cranked it, and went out to the terrace, away from the bar's booming overhead speakers. The rain was pattering on the drooping awning overhead and the night smelled like . . . like what . . . jasmine? No, that wasn't it. Something, anyway. It definitely smelled like something out here. But—

"Hey, you!" she shouted from the living room's open doorway. "There he is! There's my big stud. Come on in here, son. Let's dance! Waltz your ass on in here, baby boy, right now!"

He downed his drink and went inside. Crystal stood in the center of the room wearing a skintight S&M outfit. A black leather bodysuit that would have put Catwoman to shame. She had little Rikki Nelson cuddled atop her bulging tits, nuzzling her with kisses.

"Where's the whip, kitten?" he said.

"Oh, I'll dig one up somewhere, don't worry."

Harding collapsed into the nearest armchair and stared.

"Why are you staring like that at me and Rikki?" she pouted.

"Just trying to figure out whether or not that diamond-studded leash of yours is on the wrong bitch."

Give her credit, she laughed.

"I sure hope to hell you know how to dance, mister," she said. "Now get up and get with it, I mean it."

He hauled himself manfully up out of the leather chair.

You do what you have to do, he reminded himself.

And he danced.

And danced some more.

CHAPTER FOUR

He was drenched in sweat and panting like an old bird dog. Even the sheets were wet. Somehow he'd managed to give her three Big Os, two traditional and, last, one utterly exhausting one. He'd never worked so hard in his life. "Outside the box," she called it, that last one.

He managed a weak smile. "Wow, you are something else, aren't you, girl? I need a cigarette."

"No time. Back in the saddle, cowboy. You got me hot, now. This cowgirl's itching to ride!"

"Crystal, seriously. I need a little breather here."

"Don't be a pussy, Harding. Momma's waiting. Turn over."

"Oh, Christ."

He rolled over onto his back and stared at the ceiling. She took his wrists and tied them to the bedposts with two Hermès scarves she'd plucked from the bedside table.

He didn't even bother trying to fight her.

"Are you trying to kill me, or what?"

"Don't you worry yourself, baby. The Cialis will kick in any minute now."

"I don't take Cialis, Crystal."

"You do now, stud. I put two in your drink down at the lobby bar. When you bent down to pat Rikki Nelson. Remember that?"

"What? Are you kidding me? F'crissakes, Crystal . . ."

"Don't say I didn't warn you, hon. Big sex, remember? Okay, I'll get on top this time. Oh, yes . . . *somebody's* ready for Momma down there. That Cialis is a bitch, isn't it? Just think, two pills, you might have an erection lasting *eight* hours . . ."

"Listen, Crystal, you've really got to stop this . . . untie me . . . I've got a pain in my chest . . . I mean it!"

"Pussy is always the best cure for whatever ails you, son. Hang on, Momma's gonna ride this bucking bronco . . ."

"Damn it, get off! I've got a cardiac condition! Doc says I'm supposed to take it easy . . . Goddammit, I'm serious! Now my arm really hurts . . . call the doctor, Crystal. Now. They must have a house doctor on call and. . . . oh, Christ almighty, it hurts . . . do something!"

"Like what?"

"My pills! My nitro pills! They're over there in my trouser pocket. . . ."

"Hold on a sec . . ."

She reached over and picked up the bedside phone, never breaking her rhythmic stride, and asked for the hotel operator.

He must have passed out from the pain. Everything was foggy, out of focus. The room was dark, the rain beating hard against the windowpanes. Just a single lamp light from a table over in the corner.

Crystal, still naked, was sitting at the foot of the bed, smoking a cigarette and talking to the doctor in hushed tones. Her head was resting on the doctor's shoulder. He couldn't make out what they were saying. He was bathed in a cold, clammy sweat and the pain had spread from behind his breastbone into and out along his left arm. Fucking hell. His wrists were still tied to the bedposts? Was she insane?

Then he noticed something that totally weirded him out. The fucking doctor? His savior?

He was naked.

He heard a sob escape his own lips, and then a cry of pain from the phantom elephant sitting atop his chest.

"Shhh," the doctor said, getting to his feet and coming to the head of the bed to stand beside him. He put his finger to his lips and said, "Shhh," again.

"You've gotta do CPR or something, Doc," Harding croaked. "My pills! They're in the right pocket of my trousers. Please. I feel like I'm going to die . . ."

"That's because you are going to die, Harding," the man said.

"What?"

"You heard me."

"Wait. Who are you?" He squinted his eyes, but he couldn't make out the physician's features.

"Vengeance, sayeth the Lord, Harding. That's who I am. Vengeance."

"You're not a doctor. . . . You're . . ."

"Dr. Death will do for now."

"Who . . . no, you're not . . . you're somebody else. You're . . ."

"Don't you recognize me anymore, Harding? I've had a

little surgery recently. A bit of Botox. But, still, the eyes are always a dead giveaway. Look close."

"Spider?"

"Bingo."

"No, can't be . . . You're *Spider*, f'crissakes," the dying man croaked.

"Right. Spider Payne. Your old buddy. Come rain or come shine. Tonight, it's rain. Look out the window, Harding. It's goddamn pouring out there. Ever see it rain so hard?"

"Gimme a break here, Spider. What are you doing . . ."

"It's called poetic justice. A little twist of fate shall we say?"

Pain scorched Torrance's body and he arched upward, straining against his bonds, coming almost completely off the bed. He didn't think anything could hurt this much.

His old nemesis knelt on the floor by the bed and started gently stroking his hair. When he spoke, it was barely above a whisper.

"You fucked me royally, Harding. Remember that? When I needed you most? When the French government, whom you always claimed to have in your pocket, nailed my balls to the wall? Kidnapping and suspicion of murder. Thirty years to life? Ring a bell?"

"That wasn't my fault, f'crissakes! Please! You gotta help me!"

"That's my line. Help *me*. You don't get to use it. Way too late for that, I'm afraid, old soldier. You're catching the next train, partner."

"I can't . . . I can't breathe . . . I can't catch my . . ."

"This is how it works, Harding. You fucked with the wrong honchos in Moscow, buddy. *Really* wrong. Ever heard of a dude goes by the name of Uncle Joe? A dead ringer for Joe Stalin. You pissed off Putin's number one henchman in the Kremlin, compadre. He's the reason I'm here. Your ass is *mine*, pal."

"Who—"

"Doesn't matter now. It's so simple, isn't it? Judgment Day. How it all works out in the end? In that dark hour when no treason, no treachery, no bad deed goes unpunished."

"I can't . . . can't . . ."

Harding Torrance opened his eyes wide in fear and pain. And as the blackness creeped in around him, and his life ran away from him like a man fleeing a burning building, he heard Spider Payne utter the last words his brain would ever register.

"You fucked me, right? But, in the end, Crystal Meth and the old Spider, well, I guess they fucked you."

"Who's Uncle Joe?" Harding Torrance whispered with the last breath left in his body.

CHAPTER FIVE

North Haven, Maine

The bright blue waters of Penobscot Bay beckoned. Cam Hooker, buttoning up a light blue and freshly laundered Brooks Brothers shirt, paused to throw open his dressing room window. Glorious morning, all right. Sunlight sparkled on the bay, white seabirds flashed and dove above. He leaned out the window, took a deep breath of pine-scented Maine air, and assessed the morning's weather.

Fresh breeze out of the east, and a moderate chop, fifteen knots sustained, maybe gusting to thirty. Barometer falling, increased cloudiness, possible thunderheads moving in from the west by midmorning. Chance of rain showers later on, oh, sixty to seventy percent, give or take.

Perfect.

Certainly nothing an old salt like Cameron Hooker couldn't handle.

It was Sunday, praise the Lord, his favorite day of the week. The day he got to take himself, his *New York Times*, and whatever tattered paperback spy novel he was currently headlong into reading for the third time (an old Alastair

MacLean) out on his boat for a few tranquil hours of peace and quiet and bliss.

Hooker had sailed her, his black ketch *Maracaya*, every single Sunday morning of his life, for nigh on forty years now, rain or shine, sleet, hail or snow.

Man alone. A singleton. Solitary.

It was high summer again, and summer meant grandchildren by the dozen. Toddlers, rug rats, and various ragamuffins running roughshod throughout his rambling old seaside cottage on North Haven Island. *Haven?* Hah! Up and down the back stairs they rumbled, tearing roughshod through the rose gardens, dashing inside and out, darting through his vegetable patches and into his library, all the while shouting at peak decibels some mysterious new battle cry, "Huzzah! Huzzah!" picked up God knows where.

It was the victory cheer accorded to General George Washington, he knew that, but this intellectually impoverished gizmo generation had not a clue who George Washington was! Of that much, at least, he was certain.

You knew you were down in the deep severe when not a single young soul in your entire family had the remotest clue who the hell the Father of Our Country was!

In his day, portraits of the great man beamed benevolence down on students from every wall of every classroom. He was our Father, the Father of our country. *Your* country! Why, if someone had told young Cam back then that in just one or two generations, the general himself would have been scrubbed clean from our—why, he would have—

"What are you thinking about, dear?" his wife, Gillian, said, interrupting Cam's dark reverie at the breakfast table later that morning. She was perusing what he'd always referred to as the "Women's Sports Section." Also sometimes known as the bridal pages in the Sunday edition of the *New York Times*. Apparently, the definitive weekly "Who's Who" of who'd married whom last week. For all those out there who, like his wife of sixty years, were still keeping score, he supposed.

"You're frowning, dear," she said.

"Hmm."

He scratched his grizzled chin and sighed, gazing out at the tall forests of green trees marching down to the bright harbor. Even now, a mud-caked munchkin wielding a blue Frisbee bat advanced stealthily up the hill, stalking Cam's old chocolate Lab, Captain, sleeping in the foreground.

"Will you look at that?" he mused.

Gillian put the paper down and peered at him over the toaster.

"What is it, dear?"

"Oh, nothing. It's July, you know," he said, rapping sharply on the window to alert his dog and scare the munchkin away.

"July? What about it?"

"It *is* the cruelest month," he said, not looking up from the Book Review. "Not April. July. That's all."

"Oh, good heavens," she said, and snatched away her section of the paper.

Dismissed, he stood and leaned across the table to kiss his wife's proffered cheek.

"It's your own damn fault, Cam Hooker," she said, stroking his rosy cheek. "If you'd relent for once in your life, if you'd only let them have a television to watch, just one! That black-and-white set gathering dust up in the attic would do, the one you watched the Watergate thing on. Or even one of those hand-held computer thingies, whatever they're called; silence would reign supreme in this house once more. But no. Not you."

"A *television*? In this house?" he said. "Oh, no. Not in this house. Never! I'll buy more books if I have to!"

"There's no *room* for more books, Cam!"

Grabbing his newspapers, book, and canvas sail bag and swinging out into the backyard, slamming the screen door behind him, he headed down the sloping green lawn to his dock. The old Hooker property, some fifteen acres of it, was right at the tip of Crabtree Point, with magnificent views of the Fox Islands Thorofare inlet and the Camden Hills to the west. Cameron was the fifth-generation Hooker to summer on this island, not that anyone cared a whit about such things anymore. Traditions, history, common sense, and common courtesy, things like that, all gone to hell or by the wayside. Hell, they were trying to get rid of *Christmas*! Some goddamn school district in Ohio had banned the singing of "Silent Night." "Silent Night"?

Next thing you knew they'd be banning Old Glory in the goddamn schools.

He could see the old girl out there at the far end of the dock when he crested the hill. Just the sight of her never failed to move him. His heart skipped a beat, literally, every time she hove into view.

Maracaya.

She was an old Alden design ketch, and he'd owned her for longer than time. Forty feet on the waterline, wooden hull, gleaming black Awlgrip, with a gold cove stripe running along her flank beneath the gunwales. Her decks were teak, her spars were Sitka spruce, and she was about as yar as any damn boat currently plying the waters of coastal Maine, in his not-so-humble, humble opinion.

Making his way down the hill to the sun-dappled water, Cam couldn't take his eyes off her.

She'd never looked better.

He had a young kid this summer, sophomore at Yale, living down here in the boathouse. The boy helped him keep *Maracaya* in proper Bristol fashion. She was a looker, all right, but she was a goer, too. He'd won the Block Island Race on her back in '87, and then the Nantucket Opera Cup the year after that. Now, barely memories, just dusty trophies on the mantel in some peoples' goddamn not-so-humble opinion.

"Morning, Skipper," the crew-cut blond kid said, popping his head up from the companionway. "Coffee's on below, sir. You're good to go."

"Thanks, Ben, good on ya, mate."

"Good day for it, sir," the boy said, looking up at the big blue sky with his big white smile. He was a good kid, this Ben Sparhawk. Sixth-generation North Haven—his dad and granddad were both hardworking lobstermen. Came from solid Maine stock too. Men from another time, men who could toil at being a fisherman, a farmer, a sailor, a lumberman, a shipwright, and a quarryman, all rolled into one. And master of all.

Ben was a history major at New Haven, on a full scholarship. He had a head on his shoulders, he did, and he used it. He came up from the galley below and quickly moved to the port-side bow, freeing the forward, spring, and aft mooring lines before leaping easily from the deck down onto the dock.

"Prettiest boat in the harbor, sir," Ben said, looking at her gleaming mahogany topsides with some pride.

"Absofuckinlutely, son," Cam said, laughing out loud at his good fortune, another golden day awaiting him out there on the water. He was one of the lucky ones and he knew it. A man in good health, of sound mind, and looking forward to the precious balance of his time here on earth, specifically in the great state of Maine.

Cam Hooker threaded his way, tacking smartly through the teeming Thorofare. It was crowded as hell, always was this time of year, especially this Fourth of July weekend. Boats and yachts of every description hove into view: the Vinalhaven ferry steaming stolidly across, knockabouts and dinghies, a lovely old Nat Herreshoff gaff-headed Bar Harbor 30; and here came one of the original Internationals built in Norway, sparring with a Luders; and even a big Palmer Johnson stinkpot anchored just off Foy Brown's Yard, over a hundred feet long he'd guess, with New York Yacht Club burgees emblazoned on her smokestack. Pretty damn fancy for these parts, if you asked him.

As was his custom, once he was in open water, Cam had put her hard over, one mile from shore and headed for the pretty little harbor over on the mainland at Rockport. Blowing like stink out here now. Clouding up. Front moving in for damn sure. He stood to windward at the helm, both hands on the big wheel, his feet planted wide, and sang a few bars of his favorite sailor's ditty, sung to the tune of the old English ballad "Robin on the Moor":

"It was a young captain on Cranberry Isles did dwell;
He took the schooner Arnold, one you all know well.
She was a tops'l schooner and hailed from Calais, Maine;
They took a load from Boston to cross the raging main—"

The words caught in his throat.

He'd seen movement down in the galley below. Not believing his eyes, he looked again. Nothing. Perhaps just a light shadow from a porthole sliding across the floor as he fell off the wind a bit? Nothing at all; and yet it had spooked him there for a second but he—

"Hello, Cam," a strange-looking man said, suddenly making himself visible at the foot of the steps down in the galley. And then he was climbing up into the cockpit.

"What the hell?" Cam said, startled.

"Relax. I don't bite."

"Who the hell are you? And what the hell are you doing aboard my boat?"

Cam eased the main a bit to reduce the amount of heel and moved higher to the windward side of the helm station. He planted himself and bent his knees, ready for any false move from years of habit in the military and later as a special agent out in the field. The stranger made no move other than to plop himself down on a faded red cushion on the leeward side of the boat and cross his long legs.

"You don't recognize me? I'm hurt. Maybe it's the long hair and the beard. Here, I know. Look at the eyes, Cam, you can always remember the eyes."

Cam looked.

Was that *Spider*, for God's sake?

It couldn't be. But it was. Spider Payne, for crissakes. A guy who'd worked for him at CIA briefly the year before Cam had retired. Good agent, a guy on the way up. He'd lost track of him long ago . . . and now?

"Spider, sure, sure, I recognize you," Cam said, keeping his voice as even as he could manage. His right hand had started twitching involuntarily and he stuck it in the pocket of his jeans. His mind was ramped up, searching wildly for some kind of explanation as to how the hell this man came to be here. It just didn't make any damn sense at all.

"What in God's name is going on?"

"See? I knew this might freak you out. You know, if I just showed up on the boat like this. Sorry. I drove all night from Boston, then came over to the island on the ferry from Rockland last night. Parked my truck at Foy Brown's boatyard and went up to that little inn, the Nebo Lodge. Fully booked, not a bed to be had, wouldn't you know. Forgot it was the Fourth weekend. Stupid, I guess."

"Spider, you know this is highly goddamn unprofessional. Showing up like this. Uninvited. Are you all right? What's this all about?"

"How I found you, you mean?"

"*Why* you found me, Spider."

ABOUT THE AUTHOR

TED BELL, former writer-in-residence, Cambridge University, was chairman of the board and world-wide creative director of Young & Rubicam, one of the world's largest advertising agencies. He is the *New York Times* bestselling author of *Hawke, Assassin, Pirate, Spy, Tsar, Warlord, Phantom,* and *Warriors,* along with a series of YA adventure novels.

www.Facebook.com/TedBellNovels
www.tedbellbooks.com
www.witnessimpulse.com

Discover great authors, exclusive offers, and more at hc.com.